D1565155

LASSO

THE

MOON

LASSO

T · H · E

MOON

Dennis Covington

Delacorte Press

Published by
Delacorte Press
Bantam Doubleday Dell Publishing Group, Inc.
1540 Broadway
New York, New York 10036

The trademark Delacorte Press® is registered
in the U.S. Patent and Trademark Office.

Book design by Patrice Sheridan

The text of this book is set in 13 point Bembo.

Library of Congress Cataloging-in-Publication Data

Covington, Dennis.
Lasso the moon / Dennis Covington.
p. cm.
Summary: When April Hunt moves to St. Simons Island, Georgia, to live with her
father, a recovering alcoholic, she becomes involved with an illegal alien from El
Salvador and learns about his life and country.
ISBN 0-385-32101-5
[1. Alcoholism—Fiction.   2. Salvadorans—Fiction.   3. Illegal aliens—Fiction.
4. Fathers and daughters—Fiction.]   I. Title.
PZ7.C83449Las   1995

[Fic]—dc20   94-26073
                                                                              CIP
                                                                              AC

Manufactured in the United States of America

March 1995
10 9 8 7 6 5 4 3 2 1

for Ellaree Russell Covington
my mother

ACKNOWLEDGMENTS

Special thanks to Mary Cash and Rosalie Siegel; Vicki, Ashley, and Laura Covington; Catherine Hopkins; Leah and Lee Hopkins; Anne Cork; Sarah Lynn Bledsoe; Heather Crabb; Hayes Williams; Sue Murrell and the staff of the Emmet O'Neal Library; the University of Alabama at Birmingham; the friends of Bill W.; and the people I knew in El Salvador.

1

I had just brought out a horse and pony for a customer and his son. The son was an eight-year-old with big red ears and eyes like cracked porcelain. Sarah Commodore, the part owner of Commodore Stables where I work, came out of her office. "That doesn't look good," she said.

Mrs. Commodore was talking about the sky, of course, because anybody could tell there was a storm coming in from the mainland. I looked at the customer to see what he thought about his eight-year-old getting barbecued by a bolt of lightning, but he acted like he hadn't heard. That's the thing about Mrs. Commodore. She is big and beefy, but she has the tiniest voice in the world. Most of the customers just ignore her, but I have always made a special effort to listen. That's how I got this job with no experience. I listened to her life story for half the afternoon and then confessed I'd never been on a horse before. She hired me on the spot.

"That's all right, April," she said. "You'll learn."

The customer's wife was in the background chewing her fake nails to polystyrene shreds. She was wearing candy red sunglasses, and a jeans jacket over her beige turtleneck.

"I think we'd better let the Morgans reschedule," Mrs. Commodore said, but nobody but me heard her.

The boy was climbing up the steps of the mounting block. I boosted him up onto the saddle. Then I steadied his mount, a black pony named Midnite, and glanced at the sky again. It was purple and deep, like a fresh bruise. It wasn't tornado season, but it looked like this could develop into one of those freakish winter thunderstorms my dad had been telling me about. I was still new to the island, since school started in September, but I already knew about the winter thunderstorms.

"What do you think, Mr. Morgan?" Mrs. Commodore said. "I will leave it up to you."

He acted like he still hadn't heard her.

"Whatever you say, Mr. Morgan," she said with a little sigh. She had already gotten him, like all the other customers, to sign a form two pages long that exempts the stables from civil or criminal prosecution. I don't know anything about the law, but I do know that horses hate lightning.

"We can't be held accountable," she added, and finally Mr. Morgan seemed to understand. He waved her away with his hand. He was working on a humongous hangover. Close up, his face looked like a red fishnet.

I mounted Trader, my favorite horse, and flicked him with the reins, but I just knew that lightning was going to strike the live oak in the center of the ring and barbecue the boy. I could see myself recovering in the hospital. There would be flowers from all the kids at school who had made such a studied attempt to ignore me.

Actually the lightning wasn't that close, and there wasn't any thunder. Still, the low, dark clouds moving so fast above the trees were enough to spook me. The cars on the road to Fort Frederica had turned on their lights. Some of them had windshield wipers on. It must have already been sprinkling out near the cause-way.

Midnite had stalled like she always does just past the first turn in the ring, where she can catch a glimpse of the door to her stall and the hay spilt out in front of the door. She shook her head and rocked back on her haunches. The boy was working up a set of tears. I slapped Midnite on the flank, but there was no getting her to move. Mr. Morgan, meanwhile, had cantered on ahead. He was pulling up on the reins, and he had too much slack. It occurred to me then that the guy had never been on a horse before, but what room did I have to talk? This was only my third month at the stables. I was still a virgin, accord-ing to Rob Allard. He's eighteen and eaten alive by sex. You would not expect someone who grew up around horses to be so crude, but Rob says a long ride on the beach is like getting his rocks off without worrying about paternity or AIDS.

The sky lit up for an instant and there was a rumble of thunder. As I said, Mr. Morgan had cantered on ahead, sitting erect in the saddle pretending to be in control of the situation, when it was easy enough to tell that Alfred, the big pinto he was riding, was out of control. Fortunately for Mr. Morgan, out of control for Alfred was cantering doggedly in a circle with his head cocked like a lewd old man. Alfred was our oldest horse, the one we gave to the middle-aged rich men from Atlanta like Mr. Morgan. I was still trying to get Midnite to budge. Ponies are more stubborn than mules.

"Giddyap," I said, more to please the eight-year-old than to budge Midnite. Suddenly I noticed a peculiar smell in the air and the hair on my arms stood up. Then there was this flash. The thunder struck like a cracking bone and the sky rained particles of light. The silence afterward was startling, and the horses, as stunned as the rest of us, just stood there bunching up their fleshy necks before charging the fence.

I tried to yell at Trader—he always obeys voice commands—but the air was dead in my throat. He had pinned my right leg against a fence post and was starting to buck. "Whoa!" I finally yelled. His neck was rock hard, but moving under the surface like coiling snakes. I pulled hard left on the reins. He freed my leg, but then backed up against the fence, kicked it twice, and reared. Then he came down so hard I thought I might flip over his head. I held on and smacked back into the saddle. The air smelled like horse sweat and battery cables.

I caught a glimpse of Mr. Morgan stretched out in the middle of the ring with his right arm raised and wavering. His horse, Alfred, was galloping through the far turn, stirrups slapping against his belly. I had never seen Alfred gallop before. The eight-year-old was raising a single long wail, which sounded like "Maaaaa," as he held on to the neck of Midnite. "April!" I heard Mrs. Commodore call. Midnite was scurrying into the stretch by the stables, her stubby legs churning and her tail flat out like a raccoon's.

I dismounted right then, stumbled forward into the dirt, but regained my balance just enough to grab hold of Midnite's reins at the bit just as she stutter-stepped past me. She skidded in the dirt and whirled around, dragging me with her, but the boy was still hanging on when Midnite came to a stop.

"You all right?" I asked him.

His hair was sticking straight up from his fore-head. "Wow," he said. He looked like he'd never had so much fun in his life.

"We better get her back to her stall," I said, patting Midnite on the star between her ears. I knew then I'd be sore the next day. Something had pulled loose in my groin when I dismounted, and my thigh was bound to be scraped raw. I was limping a little as I led Midnite and the boy back toward his father, who was sitting up, like a dunce, against the trunk of the live oak in the center of the ring. I guess Mr.

Morgan believed the stuff about lightning not striking the same place twice. His wife, her hair all down in her face, was rummaging through his shirt pocket while Mrs. Commodore looked like she was trying to unloosen his belt.

"I'm all right," he was saying. "For godsakes, leave me alone."

"It won't take two minutes for the rescue squad to get here," Mrs. Commodore said in her little voice, but Mr. Morgan ignored her. Mrs. Morgan was struggling to get something out of his pocket. Her breath was coming out in pitiful little sobs as she wrestled the top off a bottle of pills. Heart medicine, I knew without looking, nitroglycerin, point six milligram, under the tongue. My dad is a cardiologist. Mr. Morgan's face was puffy and bloodless. Something had gone completely out of his eyes. But he opened his mouth, and Mrs. Morgan put a pill under his tongue, and almost instantly he got a little color back.

There was nothing to do but wait for a minute, until he felt strong enough to stand. I looked back over my shoulder at the traffic on the road to Fort Frederica, wondering if anybody had seen what had happened in the ring, wondering if anybody would report my moment of heroism to the St. Simons police.

The lightning had already moved past us toward the marshes, and it hadn't even started to rain yet. It was like nothing out of the ordinary had happened. Alfred and Trader had settled down and were over by the fence together, nibbling at the wild sorrel that grew between the posts. Midnite would have joined them, but the boy with porcelain eyes refused to get down from her just yet, and who could blame him? He'd remember this for the rest of his life.

When Mr. Morgan finally stood up and shook the dust from his seersucker slacks, he said, "Where's the car?"

"You let me carry that," said his wife. She must have been talking about some papers that had fallen out of his pocket. The boy had slid down off Midnite all by himself by now. He was standing next to his mother, but neither one of the adults was paying a bit of attention to him.

"If you're still feeling bad," I said, "my dad could probably see you. He's a cardiologist. We don't live far from here." I never volunteer anything, usually, but I think I was miffed at them for not even saying thanks for saving their kid. Sometimes people notice you if you let them know your father's a doctor.

"What's a cardiologist doing on the island?" Mr. Morgan said. "There's no hospital here, is there?"

"There's one in Brunswick." Brunswick is a port city across the sound.

"Huh. What's your father's name?"

"Jack Hunter," I said.

"The Jack Hunter from Atlanta?" he asked.

I nodded.

"Well, that makes sense then. Mad Jack Hunter."

They started walking toward their car, a silver BMW with a sunroof and tinted windows all the way around. Mrs. Morgan had by this time picked up the boy and given him a perfunctory peck on the cheek. It was starting to drizzle a little.

"You want me to give him a call and see if he can take a look at you?" I asked. I was pressing the point out of frustration. They were the most maddening people I'd ever met. And you meet some real types on the island.

Mr. Morgan turned on me then, and I recognized the look in his eyes. "I wouldn't go to Jack Hunter if he was the last doctor on earth," he said. "I can't believe he's still practicing medicine in this state."

"He's got his license back," I said. "And he's a darn good doctor."

But I'm not sure whether I actually said that last part, or just thought it. Anyway, words are always lost on people like the Morgans.

2

It started raining hard right as I was about to take my bike out of the shed behind the stables. Mrs. Commodore had said to take off early because of the lightning and all. I had handled it just right, she said. Rob Allard, who had just come in from the beach and had missed all the excitement, overheard and asked if I wanted him to give me a ride in his classic Corvette. He always says both words, as though classic were part of the brand name. I didn't look at him. Rob is unnaturally handsome, but he's missing something upstairs. No, I told him, I like to ride my bike in the rain. Besides, I was still on fire from what that jerk from Atlanta had said. I needed cooling off.

The rain was more than I had bargained for, though. It was icy and coming down in sheets. I should have waited till it slacked, but I wasn't thinking straight. I put on my blue jeans jacket and buttoned it all the way up to my chin and pinned my hair in back with the tortoise shell clasp Mother had given me as a going-away present.

Most everything I own is a gift from somebody. Dad bought the bicycle the day I told him I was coming to live on the island. It's a metallic blue Schwinn, a basic ten-speed, but real classy looking, I think. The raincoat I always keep in my backpack for emergencies like this one was given to me by my Atlanta friend Natalie as a kind of joke. It's like a kid's rain slicker, bright yellow and with a hood that looks like a duck's head. The bill is black and the hat part has two goofy-looking duck's eyes. I knew Rob was watching me put that on, too, and trying to think of some clever put-down. Every time Rob tries to say something clever, it comes out sounding incredibly dumb. So I was on my bike and into the rain before he could make an idiot of himself. But I was the one who felt like an idiot, pedaling down the Fort Frederica road in a driving rainstorm, dressed like a giant duck.

There's a point on the road to Fort Frederica where I always come out of myself. It's just a little rise —the island is flat as can be otherwise—right before the straightaway through the Marshes of Glynn. At the beginning of fall I saw a red-winged blackbird perched on a fence post there beside a wildflower that was the exact same shade as its wing patch. On the day I'm talking about, though, the cold rain had caused a mist to rise from the marshes. Now, our house sits on the edge of the marshes. It's not very big, kind of a two-bedroom cabin really, with a great room in the center and cantilevered redwood roofs over the bedroom wings. From the road it looks like a big bird under the trees. And on this day, as I topped that rise and the rain was lifting and the mist was coming off the marsh grass and into the trees, a shaft of sunlight struck our house like an arrow.

I parked the bike in the garage, draped my duck raincoat over it to dry, and ran through the rain to the kitchen door. Through the windows in the door I could see Dad with a patient, a dark-haired guy with his T-shirt raised in back while Dad listened to his chest. It made me furious. Dad's office was above the garage, and he had sworn he would never bring patients into the house again, even though he claimed the light in the kitchen was the best he could find. So now I had to run in the rain around to the front door. I wasn't about to embarrass myself by walking into the kitchen. The gutter above the front stoop was choked with leaves, so I got absolutely drenched, right down the back of my neck, by the overflow.

Inside I went straight to my room and changed into dry jeans and socks and an old football jersey from my school in Atlanta. The abrasion on my thigh was tender but not bad enough to put anything on it. I took out the tortoise-shell clasp and shook the rain from my hair. I went across the hall to the bathroom and slammed the door closed.

From the kitchen I could hear Dad's voice. He was speaking a mixture of Spanish and English, too loud and too slow, which meant that the patient was another one of those illegal shrimpers or fruit pickers

11

who were always showing up on our doorstep. Dad had spent his Army days at a military hospital in Panama and had never gotten over it. I had grown up listening to pointless stories about iguanas and Zonies (who are the people that live in the Canal Zone), and there's a photo of Dad and his buddies at the Canal, clowning around in their tropical-weight khakis while behind them a ship the size of Cleveland moves through the locks.

"No, you go on and finish your juice," he was saying. "I'll be right back. *Con su permiso,*" he added, which means excuse me or something in Spanish.

And there he was in the hall on his way to the bathroom before I could get back to my room.

"Hey," he said. "You scared me. I didn't know you'd come in."

"The kitchen was occupied," I said, squeezing past him. He's a big man with thinning hair.

I closed the door behind me. I was all knotted up inside. The Morgans were the main reason, dragging everything I'd hated about Atlanta into my day. My thigh still hurt, and I swear I must have pulled a ligament in my groin, but there had been nobody to tell all this to. This is a problem with having a doctor for a father. You have to make a choice. Do you want the time you're with him spent going over your aches and pains? He hears that from everybody else all day. Or do you endure your own discomforts in silence? I had always kept my mouth shut and was probably dying of some terminal disease.

It startled me when I saw the boy race past my

window with his jacket over his head. The marshes behind him were as gray as the sky, and his T-shirt was white against that. Thank God I was already dressed.

"Wait a minute, Fernando!" I heard Dad call. "You can't go all the way in the rain. We'll give you a ride!"

And I saw the boy scurry back again.

*'We'*ll give you a ride.' I should have known what that meant before I heard the knock at my door.

"Uh, look, April," he began. "Do you mind? I hate to ask you, but I've got Mrs. Silkin scheduled. She's broken out in hives."

"Where does he live?"

"He's going back to work."

"Where does he work?"

"The resort."

"I just came from over that way."

"I know, but it's raining like cats and dogs."

"I rode home in the rain."

"I know, sweetheart. Sorry to bother you . . ."

"Oh, come on. Just give me the keys."

"You don't mind?" He was smiling his member-of-a-healing-profession smile. He knew I minded.

On the way down the hall, he put his arm on my shoulder. "Mrs. Silkin always brings a pie."

"A boy from Atlanta almost lost it today in the ring," I said.

"No kidding. Anybody we know?"

"They'd heard of you," I said, but he ignored my tone of voice.

"I can't tell you how much I appreciate this," he said, dragging a green umbrella from underneath a pile of summer clothes in the hall closet.

"Fernando, April. April, Fernando."

The boy looked like all the rest of them. He was thin and dour, his eyes the color of potting soil. It's impossible to tell their ages, you know.

"You take the umbrella," I said to him real loud and slow, in case he couldn't understand me. "I like to walk in the rain."

Even with the divorce and the expense of keeping two places up, you'd think Dad could have bought a decent car. I suppose a white Chevy station wagon fit his needs. It sure didn't make any kind of statement that I'd want attributed to me.

It was easy to forget where I was going or why. Fernando hadn't made a sound. I hate small talk, but the silence was starting to get to me.

"So where are you from?" I finally asked. We were making the turn at the airport, and the windshield wipers were going to beat the band.

"El Salvador," he said.

I'd heard of it, of course, because of the war there, but I had no idea where it was.

"That's an island, isn't it?"

"No."

"With lots of jungles?"

He didn't say anything, but I could tell I'd struck out again.

"Been here long?" I asked.

"A few months."

"Your English is really good."

"It's pretty bad, but thank you anyway. Do you speak Spanish?"

"No," I said. "I mean, I can say hello and good-bye."

I glanced at him and noticed the scar that ran behind his ear and down his neck. He was pressed up against his door like he couldn't wait to get out of the car.

We were coming up on the stables, and the red light caught us. There were some customers waiting in their cars for the rain to slack. "That's where I work," I said. "What do you do at the resort?"

"I'm a gardener," he said. The light changed to green.

Luckily it wasn't much farther to the resort, just that stretch of what we call the other causeway, across to Sea Island. It's such a pretty stretch, the canopy of trees opening onto a view of the marshes and the ocean way off. It had stopped raining. Just as we crossed the little bridge, the sun came out. On our left was the resort's marina, filled with bobbing sail-boats, their sails lashed to the mains. On our right was the sound, its waves gentle and regular.

There were speed breakers once we hit Sea Island, and the grounds of the resort were stately and green in a way that nothing on St. Simons is. Rob Allard told me once how much it costs per night during the season. I've forgotten the exact rate, but I couldn't believe there were people who would pay that much

15

to stay somewhere near where I live. "It's not the place," Rob said, "it's the service and the total environment." Uh-huh. "I still think it must be a rip-off," I answered.

Fernando pointed out the service road to take. It led to a greenhouse by a cleverly camouflaged Dempsey Dumpster. He already had his hand on the door handle before we pulled to a stop.

"It was nice meeting you," I said.

"The same," he said, nodding.

"Does the place you're from in El Salvador have a name?"

"It's called El Paraíso," he said.

"What's that mean?"

"Paradise."

Paradise. I pictured angels with orchids in their hair. That was the first mistake I made.

3

People think it never gets cold on St. Simons. Boy, are they wrong. It was so cold the next morning each blade of grass in the marshes was encased in a separate sheath of ice. A record low for the eighteenth of December. I called Mrs. Commodore to make sure the stables would be opened, and she said why sure, it wasn't at all cold to the Yankees staying at the resort. They'd booked the ring all morning and Rob Allard was taking the usual groups on beach trail rides. Could I bring her a thermos of black coffee? she asked. The power was out on account of a live oak branch that had fallen across the wires on the road to Fort Frederica. When I hung up, Dad, who had over-heard, insisted I take the station wagon.

"Were you able to get him to open up?" he asked over scrambled eggs and a wedge of Mrs. Silkin's chocolate chess pie.

"Why? Was I supposed to?"

"No. I just figured he would. You have a way of making people feel comfortable."

This was not entirely a lie.

"What's his problem?" I asked, although I wasn't sure I wanted to know.

"He fainted at work. Rea Britt brought him over, but had to leave him without a ride back. She apologized profusely."

Rea Britt was in public relations at the resort and went to our church. "Why didn't she take him to Brunswick?"

"He doesn't have health insurance."

A familiar story. Almost none of Dad's patients did. "You'd think the resort could at least cough up money for that, wouldn't you?" I said. I was standing at the counter waiting for the coffee to finish dripping so I could pour Mrs. Commodore her thermos.

"It's not so easy," Dad said. "Even though he works at the resort, he's employed by an independent contractor. Besides, he's here illegally."

I heated the carafe in the microwave before I poured it into the thermos. Mrs. Commodore liked it scalding.

"He's got a presystolic murmur," Dad said, more to himself than to me, "but I don't know whether that's connected to the fainting spell or not. There are so many other problems you see with refugees—incipient malaria, anemia . . ."

I knew I didn't want to hear this.

"The reason I was examining him in the kitchen was that I needed the best light I could find. There

18

are certain parasites you can only detect as they swim across the whites of the eyes . . ."

Oh, my God, I thought. "Got to run," I said.

"Whoa. It's only six-thirty."

"Mrs. Commodore has to have her caffeine fix. Power's out at the stables."

"How come I see less of you now than when school was in session?" he asked.

I promised I'd be back by four and kissed the top of his head where his scalp was freckled under his thinning hair. Middle-aged men require an inordinate amount of care, I thought.

The heater didn't even start to put out till I pulled up at the stables. I was sick I had forgotten my gloves, but glad I'd remembered my sunglasses. The sun wasn't even up good, but because of the clarity of the air, it was going to be unbearably bright. Before I went inside, I patted Trader and stroked his neck. I'd forgiven him for getting spooked by lightning and pinning me against the fence. His breath rose like plumes of smoke, and I noticed his coat was freshly groomed and his stall swept, with a stack of fresh hay in the corner.

For all his faults, Rob was at least dependable about work. He always showed up before anyone else and took his chores twice as seriously as I did. Maybe that made up for his goofing off the rest of the day. I had told him he was never going to get anywhere with the spoiled daughters of the rich people who stayed at the resort on Sea Island, but that didn't stop him from making a fool of himself every chance he got. I don't know what he saw in them anyway. It seems to me that beauty in a woman is inversely proportionate to her parents' annual income. The debutantes who went to my school in Atlanta, for instance, all looked like they'd just eaten something that didn't agree with them. The sexiest girls at the school were the ones who lived in the duplexes by the airport. Their fathers were probably unemployed. Their mothers probably worked in dry cleaning establishments.

I guess I'm somewhere in between. People tell me I don't look like a doctor's daughter. I take it as a compliment. What they mean is that I don't look like a *successful* doctor's daughter. I *do* look like the daughter of a doctor who's lost his license, his wife, and his four-hundred-thousand-dollar home in the suburbs of Atlanta, and who now practices medicine on old women and Latin American refugees at the edge of a marsh practically for free.

"Where'd you get the shades?" Rob asked me. He was warming his hands by a kerosene heater that Mrs. Commodore had brought in because of the power outage.

"They were a gift," I said, taking them off. I'd gotten them from my last Atlanta boyfriend, a boy named Zeke who wanted to be a chemist and played tuba in the All-City band.

"Thanks for taking care of Trader this morning," I said. It hurt to be nice to Rob.

"No skin off my back. You've got the ponies."

"Oh yeah. I forgot." I left the thermos of coffee on Mrs. Commodore's desk. There was no telling where she was, probably filling the bird feeder out back. Then I found the pitchfork and shovel in the utility shed. I'd come back later for a flake of fresh hay.

The thing about ponies is that you think, because they're tiny and cute, that they're also going to be clean and neat. This is not the case. I'd rather clean a row of stallions' stalls than one shared by a pair of ponies. They foul their place more often, and then they seem to get a kick out of smearing it around with their hooves. In general, I do not mind the smell of horse manure, as long as it's not absolutely fresh or smeared. If it's intact and has had a moment to sit in the cold air, forking it up is not nearly so bad as scrubbing a toilet bowl. Manure and hay and horse sweat combined are even, to me, a pleasant kind of smell. I associate it with flannel and winter and open skies. It takes everything I've got to not let Rob Allard ruin it for me. "Ah yes, the aroma of the stable," he has said, trying to imitate a comedian he's only seen imitations of. "Almost better than the smell of sex."

He's the only thing I don't like about working at the stables. Him and customers like Mr. Morgan. When you have a job like mine, most rich people just ignore you, so I don't really have problems with them. But then, every once in a while, along comes a Mr. Morgan who tries to kick you open.

I rolled the wheelbarrow down the creaking

wooden floor and out into the yard. I dumped the contents of the wheelbarrow into the manure pile and spread the stuff out and turned it over with the rusted pitchfork. Mrs. Commodore hadn't seen me. She was on her tiptoes by the horse trailer, trying to rehang her bird feeder.

I reloaded the wheelbarrow with fresh wood shavings from the lean-to by the utility shed. It may have been then, on my way back to the ponies' stall, that I noticed the boy standing along the far fence out by the road. It was hard to tell who he was for sure. I was looking down the length of the dark barn into that square of brilliant sunshine at the far end, but I suspected even then it was Fernando.

Maybe for that reason, I took my time unloading the new shavings and spreading them. I was methodical, too, with the hay, not just pitching it in like normal. And when I took the ponies' brushes and combs down from the pegs in the wall, I stopped and looked at them for a minute.

" 'To be or not to be,' " said Rob Allard. He kicked the gate shut behind me, but it just swung back on its hinges.

I started brushing Midnite hard.

"Did you read the part where he puts his head in Ophelia's lap?" Rob said.

"No, did you?"

"Of course not. I told you I got the video. I've been falling asleep to it every night. It's really not a bad story."

"I don't intend to read it," I said. The truth was, I

already had, but I didn't want to get into any more of a conversation about it with Rob. I was working on Midnite's withers now. Her widening eyes reminded me that I needed to go a little easier on her.

"You don't need to read it," Rob said. "You've got the class sewn up. Mr. Noonan thinks you're a number."

"Will you please shut up?"

"I'm just kidding," he said. "I mean, I don't care for Noonan much. I think he's probably got a ballerina on his pillowcase. Why do we have to keep the same teacher anyway?"

"Don't ask me."

"It's not right to assign us reading over the holidays."

"Don't do it then."

"I'm not."

"Neither am I."

"So I guess you got a load of your first customer."

I looked up. I had begun to work up a sweat. "He's not a customer."

"You know him?"

"He's a patient of my father's."

Rob fell silent. I could tell he was trying to figure that one out.

"I bet I know what it is," he said. "You're not going to read the play because you don't like vulgar language."

"What is it with you?" I said.

Midnite reached her head around and nudged me in the thigh. I let her nuzzle my free hand. I was

23

almost finished with the brushing, and if Rob would just leave me alone, I'd get a little enjoyment out of grooming the other pony.

"Mrs. Commodore said to forget about Xerxes," Rob said. "We've already got customers showing up."

"Is that what you came back here to tell me?"

"No, I just figured you'd be interested to know that your boyfriend was waiting to see you."

I like to think of myself as a good person, really. I'm generous; even when I was a kid, I shared candy with classmates I couldn't stand the sight of. Dad thinks I'm his angel of mercy (if anybody ever needed one, of course, it's him). Mother respects me, in her way. Mrs. Commodore tells me I am the daughter she never had. But occasionally, I do something unspeakably rotten, like that day I saw Fernando at the fence and ignored him.

Believe me, it wasn't easy. He was conspicuous against the trunks of the bare trees. His arms were crossed on top of the second rail, and he was resting his chin on them. His unzipped blue jacket rode up in back. All he was wearing underneath was a T-shirt. I had not remembered him as being so short, probably because up close his thinness gave the impression of height. At this distance, though, he looked like an only slightly overgrown child, his arms too long for the sleeves of his jacket, but his jeans too long for his legs.

The first customers that morning were two

twelve-year-old girls who had been dropped off by one of their mothers while she had her hair done. They knew more about horses than I did. They didn't need me tailing after them in the ring, so I had to invent things to do to look occupied. I dismounted and made numerous adjustments to the length of Trader's stirrups. I checked the water trough and re-filled it even though it didn't need refilling. In short, I did everything I could think of to avoid making eye contact with Fernando. And when I had exhausted all my possibilities and looked up toward the back fence, resigned to say hello, he had already disappeared.

I felt an odd mixture of shame and relief. Darn, I thought, I can't be responsible for the whole world.

"Hey, mine won't gallop!" one of the twelve-year-olds yelled to me from across the ring. Unluckily for her, she'd drawn Alfred.

I rode over to her and explained that the horses weren't allowed to gallop in the ring anyway. What she needed to do was go on one of the beach rides. Give her a few more years and Rob would probably let her go free, although I didn't say that of course.

"When's the next one?" she asked, shielding her eyes against the sun.

"Ten o'clock," I said. "But it's expensive."

The girl shrugged and looked away, as if I should have known expense was never an issue where she came from.

It was lucky for me that I went into the barn with the girls to help them sign up for the beach ride. Otherwise, I never would have noticed that the ten o'clock slot in the ring had been reserved for the Morgans again.

"What's the matter with you?" Rob asked. He was wiping mud from his boots and pretending not to be sizing up the twelve-year-olds.

"Those crazy people from Atlanta are signed up for ten o'clock," I said. "I can't handle them again. What about letting me take the beach ride?"

"You ever done it before?"

"No."

"So who'd take the ring?"

"You, if you don't mind."

"I don't do the ring anymore."

"How about making an exception today?" I asked in my most ingratiating voice.

He glanced at the girls again, his hopes dashed anyway by the fact that they were only twelve. "What the hell," he said. "Do whatever you want."

There were three cancellations after all because of the cold, so the only ones on the beach ride were me and the twelve-year-olds and a retired couple from Canada—we call them snowbirds. I let the girls go on ahead once we got to the beach, even though I probably shouldn't have. They seemed to know what they were doing. The Canadians held back and asked me a lot of questions, about the birds and the vegetation. I didn't think I knew much to tell them, but I discovered I knew more than I thought I did. For instance, I recognized the call of a killdeer, and I told the Canadians he shouldn't have been around this far into the season. They seemed pleased by this bit of information. But actually what they really wanted was to tell me the story of their lives. The horseback ride was simply an occasion for the telling of it, so I listened and asked questions. The stories the Canadians told were kind of entertaining.

The beach trail follows the other causeway, the one out to Sea Island, at just enough distance that if the wind is off the sound and carrying the noise of the cars away from you, you forget you're anywhere near civilization. Only at the bridge do you realize again where you are. The two girls had waited for us at the water, their cheeks flushed from the cold air, and because the tide was out the horses were able to wade across.

Then I realized how close we would be coming to the resort. We would be passing literally feet from where some of the sailboats were moored at the marina. Even as the thought occurred to me that I might see Fernando again, I did. He was stopped in front of the sea wall, planting a japonica. His back was to the beach, and he didn't turn around. We continued past him up the beach to the point where the sand ends in a rocky jetty and a no trespassing sign. On our way back, Fernando happened to stand up and turn toward the beach just as we were passing. I couldn't read his expression, but I smiled and waved at him. He nodded and turned back to his work.

In this way I redeemed myself, but I had made sure it was on his turf and not my own.

4

"Does he have family on the island?" I asked Dad after dinner.

"He has a sister in Los Angeles."

"How'd he end up here?"

"You'd have to ask him."

"I don't want to ask him. I'll probably never see him again. I'm just curious."

It was Dad's turn to do the dishes, but I couldn't seem to stay away from the sink. Our dishwasher was broken, and I had always suspected that Dad didn't get all the soap off when he rinsed.

"Why don't you just let me finish these?" I said.

"Why don't you just relax?"

I hate it when people tell me to relax. I got a sponge and started wiping off the stove top and counter. "It's just strange that a boy that young could wind up a thousand miles from home without anybody seeming to know or care."

"A boy that young? How old do you think he is?" Dad asked.

"How old is he?"

"Nineteen."

"You've got to be kidding," I said.

"That's what he told me."

"Well, I don't believe that. I don't think he's over fifteen. Did you notice how thin his wrists were?"

Dad didn't have to answer, it was such a stupid question. He knew what Fernando's blood sounded like as it left his heart. He had pondered the color of the skin beneath his nails.

"The average Salvadoran eats less protein than the average North American house cat," he explained.

"I think he's a little bit weird," I said suddenly without knowing why.

"In what way?"

The washed dishes were stacking up on the drainboard, so I abandoned the sponge and got a dish towel and started drying them. "He's too quiet."

"That's true, but not exactly a sign of weirdness."

"It's just a gut feeling," I said.

I could feel Dad's eyes on me as he started on the baking dish that he'd left to soak. I hadn't told him that Fernando had showed up at the stables at sunrise or that I'd seen him on Sea Island later.

"Maybe you're right," he said. "You're a pretty good judge of character."

"Maybe weird is not the word," I said, and waited. "What's it like down there?" I meant Central America, and I knew this was a risky question. If I

29

wasn't careful, he'd have the album down with the photos of him and his friends in Panama, and I'd have to endure for the umpteenth time the stories like the one about Colonel Abrahms's housekeeper and the iguana that fell into the bean soup.

Dad rinsed the baking dish and put it in the drainboard. "El Salvador is very beautiful. Very poor." That was all he said.

"He comes from a town that means paradise."

"El Paraíso," he said. "I know the place. God, I could use a drink."

I ignored that. He said it about as often and with as little conscious thought as a normal person might say "God bless you" after a sneeze.

"Rea's driving him to Jacksonville for tests," Dad said. "Fernando," he reminded me. "The Salvadoran."

"I'm listening," I said. I hadn't been.

"I told her it might be nice to have them stop by on Christmas Eve."

"You what?"

"I told her I'd ask you first. It's nothing definite."

"I've got to check on the horses for the Commodores. They'll be out of town, visiting their son. She left me the key."

"I know. You told me that," he said.

"Besides, I thought we were holing up here without seeing anybody until the day after Christmas?"

"That's fine," he said. "I'll explain that to her. Case closed."

"What's the deal with Rea and this guy anyway?" I asked.

"He lives upstairs in her house, where her mother lived before she died." He dried his hands and poured himself a glass a water. "Don't mention that to anyone, of course."

"Who would I mention it to?"

Dad smiled. He set down the empty glass and began wrapping foil around some leftovers he'd forgotten about. The dishes put away, Dad went into the great room and turned on the TV. I walked to the window, but couldn't see much of the marsh because of the reflected hall light in the glass. I felt like I was coming out of my skin. You'd think living on the island would have calmed me down. I thought it would lower my pulse rate, that I'd be watching birds all the time, but instead I was watching myself come loose at the seams.

Then a terrible thought hit me. Maybe I *missed* Dad's drinking. Maybe I missed the meanness, the unpredictability. Something was always about to happen in those days. In normal people's houses, supper was on the table at six. They microwaved popcorn and played cards and watched TV. I know because I spent the night with normal people sometimes. The adults went to bed at ten. In our house, supper was anybody's guess. It might be a pizza with peppers and black olives that showed up cold at eleven, the delivery boy freezing and afraid at the front door. Sometimes it would end up on the wall.

Even when Dad said he was trying to quit, I

could smell it on him, sometimes whiskey, sometimes beer. When he drank only beer, Mother would say he was off the sauce, and shouldn't we be happy, because he wasn't drinking the hard stuff anymore. For a while he got onto a tequila craze, and he made a big production of mixing margaritas in a blender. Mother called this "getting hold of his drinking," because he was only drinking drinks that he made in a blender.

And then there were the times when Mother said he had quit drinking altogether. This was when he only drank wine with meals, the way normal people did, according to Mother. The pattern never changed, though. After a couple of whatever he was drinking, he'd start to get a little pink-faced and kind of funny and affectionate. And after a couple more, he'd start talking loud and philosophically about what he called the great questions of our day, and after a couple more he'd get real sloppy and sentimental, and repeat himself. After that, he'd just get mean. Then there came a time, after the meanness, when it didn't much matter who he was or what he did. He wouldn't remember it the next day anyway. One night he put his fist through a window and had to get stitches. Another time he tried to microwave our cat.

Almost every Saturday night I went to bed to the sound of a nonsensical argument. I would hold off sleep waiting for the climax, the sound of broken glass or a slamming door or Mother bursting into tears (she made a high-pitched, hysterical shriek when she broke down completely, like I imagine a horse makes when his stall is on fire). On more than one occasion, the police had shown up. Could I possibly have been missing all that?

"Why don't you grab a chair?" Dad said.

"No thanks."

"Restless?"

"Yeah."

"Take the wagon," he said. "We need a few things at the store."

I sat down beside him anyway. The program he was watching was a special report about homelessness. My eyes began to sting.

"What's wrong, April?" he said.

"I don't know." I fought it back.

"Do you miss your mother?"

I shook my head. She was in Spain until January with a friend of hers.

"Is it me?"

"Please. I'm okay."

"Okay. I didn't mean to pry."

That wasn't it. I wanted him to pry. "Do you have a list?" I asked. I tried not to sniff audibly.

"No, but I think we need the usual things. Don't forget the toilet paper and Comet cleanser."

"Okay."

"And eggs."

"Medium?"

He nodded. I went to get my windbreaker and the joint checkbook. He was standing by the fireplace when I came out. "That boy Fernando said something funny to me the other day," he said. "I haven't been able to shake it."

I pulled the windbreaker over my head.

"I was just trying to think of small talk while I checked his blood pressure," Dad continued. "I asked him what he did for pleasure."

"So what'd he say?"

"He said he didn't know what I meant."

"Did he understand the question?"

"Oh yeah, he understands English plenty well enough. It was the concept of pleasure he didn't seem to grasp."

5

I ran into Rea Britt in frozen foods, next to the fruit popsicles. She was wearing jeans and a sweatshirt with Wolftrap Music Festival on the front. I hope I look as good at her age, able to wear whatever I want. She did not seem surprised to see me. The island is small, after all, and gets smaller the longer you live here.

Rea gave me a strong, two handed shake. "I'm glad to see you safe and sound."

I didn't know what she meant.

"Sarah Commodore told me what a close call you had the other day," she explained. "I didn't catch all the details."

"It wasn't a big deal."

"You couldn't catch me dead on a horse," she said. "How's Jack?"

"Fine. He's at home watching the news."

Rea leaned into her cart and tightened the corners of her mouth, as though she were considering something. "You might tell Jack for me that I got a call from the I.N.S."

"The I.N.S.?"

"The Immigration and Naturalization Service. It was not about anyone in particular, just some general questions about the presence on the island of undocumented refugees." She looked up at me. "I guess they called me because the resort is the largest employer and I'm the official spokesperson. It did catch me a little off balance, though."

I didn't know why she was telling me this. She could have called Dad just as easily.

"I didn't volunteer any information. Tell Jack that. He may be getting a call soon, too."

"What do you think they'll do to him?"

"To Jack? Why nothing."

"No, to Fernando," I said.

Rea lowered her voice as a stock boy passed us pushing a pallet of canned peaches. "If they get wind of him, I'm sure they'll try to deport him," she said. She motioned me to follow as she headed down the aisle toward the checkout lanes. We strolled side by side, although I knew I would have to go back for the eggs.

"It would be terrible if they sent Fernando back to El Salvador," she said.

"Couldn't he find a job there, too?"

"That's not the issue. Fernando says they'll kill him."

"Who?"

Rea shrugged. "I don't claim to understand the politics of the place, April. I just know that I believe him. If he says he'll be killed, I'm sure he has reason to fear it." She smiled despite what she had just said, and I realized I'd have to find out what El Salvador was really like. "I hope you have a chance to get to know him better," she said. "He doesn't seem to have any friends he can trust. He's a very generous person, very direct. Troubled, of course, but who wouldn't be under the circumstances?" We had reached the line at the register by then, and Rea signaled with her eyes that this part of our conversation was over. "What's Santa Claus bringing you?" she asked.

Old Santa Claus. I hadn't given him a thought. "Switches, I guess."

She smiled. "Somehow I doubt that."

"I forgot some stuff," I said apologetically. "I guess I'll see you later." And I kicked the wheels of my cart to get it started in the right direction.

"I'm glad we ran into each other," she called after me. "I still want you to have lunch with me sometime at the resort. The food is out of this world."

"I'd like that," I said, and I surprised myself by meaning it.

"Mum's the word," she reminded me.

I gave a little wave and headed back up the aisle toward the dairy products. At the frozen vegetables case, I glanced back around. Rea was waiting patiently in line, not even thumbing through the gossip magazines like I would have been. I worried about her. I worried about myself. I wondered what I would do if I was her age, with no children, never been married, both parents dead, and living alone in a house too big for me with a foreigner sleeping upstairs.

6

If I hadn't known better, I would have thought there was something going on between Dad and Rea Britt. They weren't conspiratorial or anything; it's just that they had a way of enduring silence together. After church, for instance, standing around in the vestibule waiting for the rain to slack, they didn't seem compelled to make the kinds of small talk that everyone else made.

When I first came to the island, I asked Dad if he didn't think Rea was attractive. She is, in fact, the tallest woman I have ever seen in person. He said he thought she was very attractive, but he said it as though he'd never really considered the question before.

The only information that Dad has volunteered is that Rea is a recovering alcoholic like himself. I'm not supposed to know that, of course, but Dad always tells me more than I'm supposed to know. They don't go to the same A.A. meetings. He goes to the one at the American Legion Post in the village. Rea goes to Epworth community center. (Dad can tolerate cigarette smoke; she can't.) But they seem to know one another in a way that nobody else around here does, as though they'd grown up together.

On the Thursday before Christmas, Rea drove Fernando to Jacksonville for his echocardiogram, which is like an X ray of the heart, except that it's done with sound. Fernando had to go to Jacksonville because the hospital in Brunswick didn't have the machine that does the test. The procedure's real expensive, which is why we took up a special offering at church to cover some of the cost. Without naming names, Dad had suggested to the board of stewards that the church join the Sanctuary movement and take in Latin American refugees. The old families in the church vetoed that. Paying for an echocardiogram for an unnamed Salvadoran refugee was a way to save face, I guess.

I had not seen Fernando since he'd come to the stables, but I couldn't stop thinking about him. I imagined what El Paraíso, his town in El Salvador, must have been like. The name itself held a kind of magic for me, the first words in Spanish I'd wanted to know more about. I'd had a year of Spanish at my old high school in Atlanta before I switched to French, which also didn't interest me. But now I tried to find El Paraíso in Dad's atlas. El Salvador was nothing, a sliver of land on the underbelly of Central America. Only three towns appeared on the map—San Salvador, the capital; one in the west, Santa Ana; and one in the east, San Miguel.

The old travel books at the St. Simons library were not much help either. All the books about Latin America focused on Mexico or Argentina or Brazil. Sometimes Peru, because of the Incas. If mention was made of Central America, it was always about Guatemala or Costa Rica. I thought I'd hit the jackpot when I found a *National Geographic* with an article called "Salvador: Where Carnival Is a Year-Round Affair," but it was about a city called Salvador in the Bahia region of Brazil. And there was a third Salvador, I discovered, an island in the Caribbean, which may have been a paradise all right, but not the right one.

El Paraíso. I would have to invent my own. What I imagined were whitewashed houses that cast shadows in the afternoon. There was no traffic, only the sound of doves and the peal of a church bell on Sundays and an occasional guitar. Nobody worked. Pomegranates and oranges could be picked off the trees. There were flowers along the courtyard walls. The men removed their hats when they passed and called you *señorita*. During fiestas there were fireworks above the rooftops. And everyone, I imagined, in El Paraíso, even the children and old women, rode a horse.

I knew none of this was so, but that didn't matter. I have this thing about places. What they suggest to me is more important than what they are. Before I left the library, though, I copied a bunch of articles out of news magazines and some from *The New York Times,* which the library's got on microfilm. Right as I was leaving, I finally thought to ask Mrs. Whiting, at the front desk, and she told me about a book called *Salvador,* by a woman named Joan Didion, that the library didn't have but that Mrs. Whiting thought I could get in paperback at the bookstore in the village. She was right. So I took all the copies of articles and the Didion book and even some of the travel books that were mostly about Guatemala and Costa Rica, and I stacked them in a corner of my room next to my bed, thinking I might get around to reading them late at night, after Dad had gone to bed. In the meantime, I had my imagination.

I think that's what I ended up wanting to tell Fernando that afternoon when he and Rea Britt stopped by on their way back from Jacksonville. I wanted to say, I am an exile, too, in my imagination. But of course I didn't. I got a closer look at him this time, though. I still didn't believe he was nineteen. His skin was dark and smooth, like a boy's who's been playing outside all summer, and his eyes were totally uncomplicated, but there was something in the way he held back at the door, not shyness, but reserve, that told me he was older than he looked.

"Buenas tardes. Cómo están?" Dad said. He patted Rea's hand and shook Fernando's formally. I shook his hand, too, hoping he wouldn't do something embarrassing like kiss me on the cheek. His skin was dry and cool; he smelled like cinnamon.

42

Rea had just had her hair done. It was short and blond and brushed back from her temples. Her bangs had a ragged, casual look. I think the overall effect was supposed to be professional but not too serious about it, kind of the way I felt about Rea herself.

"I thought you'd be at the stables," she said.

"I'm going by there later on."

"Sit down, sit down," Dad said. *"Siéntense, por favor."*

"His Spanish is really good," Fernando said to Rea, and I'll be darned if Dad didn't blush.

"I just hung up with Cohen in Jacksonville," Dad said.

"So what's the word?" Rea asked.

Dad looked first at Fernando and then back at Rea. She and I were sitting on the sofa, Fernando in a chair to my right that faced the marsh, Dad in another chair in front of us. I could see Fernando's scar.

"As I suspected, Fernando's got a minor problem with one of the valves in his heart." Dad leaned forward and began doing things with his hands, molding a kind of three dimensional heart in the air. "The valve that separates the left atrium and left ventricle is constricted." He made a funnel shape with one of his hands. "The heart has to work too hard to pump the blood. The condition is called mitral stenosis. It probably sounds worse than it is. It'll have to be watched, but Cohen doesn't think it's that bad right now."

"Will he have to have surgery?" Rea asked.

"No. Not unless the valve deteriorates further.

You've got your prescription, right?" he asked Fernando, who nodded.

"Even if you do have to have surgery down the road, it'll be fairly routine. The outcome is almost always good."

Fernando glanced at me, a brief, impersonal glance, like a lighthouse swinging its beam around.

"So the important thing now is to take the medication Cohen prescribed and stop by here occasionally and let me listen to your heart. You want to be sure you let me know if you have any more fainting spells or start running a high fever. There's always a danger of the valve getting infected, and that really could be serious."

I must have phased out on the sense of the conversation then; it was only the sound that mattered, the music of sober adults. I liked being close to Rea. I had felt comfortable in her presence from the start, and if there *had* been something going on between her and Dad, I don't think I would have minded.

Dad and I ate out that night, something we hardly ever did. It was the Mexican restaurant over by the airport. I had an enormous taco salad with guacamole sauce. Dad had the beef enchiladas and refried beans. The intention of the decor was to make you think you were really in Mexico, all that tile, and the serapes and sombreros on the walls. But I had insisted on a window booth where I could see the live oaks and the beacon on the airport tower through the rain.

Even in a franchised Mexican restaurant, I figure I can be on the St. Simons of my imagination.

"What do you hear from your mother?" Dad asked.

"They're in the Pyrenees."

"She seems to have gotten her life in order rather nicely," Dad said. It had been two years since the divorce, but he still talked like that.

"Yeah, maybe she'll settle down with somebody who knows how to take care of things," I said.

He smiled. It was our one joke about his drinking. After everything he'd done to Mother, locking her out of the house during an ice storm, chipping both her front teeth, not to mention the concussion and the ruined silk dress and all the rest, that was the only complaint she had cited in the papers her lawyer filed; he "didn't know how to take care of things."

"You're going to like the dessert," he said.

It was flan with caramel. Mother and I had eaten it at the Hyatt Regency in Atlanta, one time when she moved out of the house and took me with her. She said we were going to stay with her sister in Augusta, but we wound up at the Hyatt Regency for four days. We never talked about why she left the house, or why we wound up at the Hyatt Regency instead of Aunt Audrey's. I was twelve then and decided not to look a gift horse in the mouth. We had room service deliver breakfast every morning and we swam until noon, until the shadows of the buildings in Peachtree Center chilled the pool. Then Mother got a body massage after a vegetable buffet lunch and I curled up in the double poster bed with a book by S. E. Hinton, the volume off on MTV, and the sunlight streamed through the mini-blinds and left a pattern on the wall. At night we'd eat light, fruit salad and flan. Then one morning we just checked out and went straight home. Mother charged it all to her gold Visa card. But we never told Dad or anyone else where we'd really been those four days, and so I acted like I knew Aunt Audrey better than I did and like I'd never had flan before.

"Cohen thinks the mitral insufficiency is within tolerable limits."

I looked up at him. He dabbed at his chin with his napkin. "Fernando," he said.

"I heard all about his heart. I just don't know what any of it means."

"Oh." He scratched the line of his jaw and then his neck. His fingers seemed whiter and more delicate than they had before he dried out. In general his color had improved, of course. He'd lost that puffy corpselike fat most drunks carry around and the perpetual high color in his nose and cheeks.

"Well, it's nothing to be too concerned about right now," Dad said. "Fernando's actually in pretty good health otherwise."

I didn't want him to go into details, and he didn't. Occasionally he told me too much about patients, without being aware that he was doing anything other than thinking out loud. There is something painfully intimate about doctors and their patients. It had always aroused an emotion like jealousy in me. I'd never told anyone that either. I was just now beginning to realize how many things there were that I hadn't ever told anyone about.

7

(Christmas Eve was the darkest night of the year.
(Nobody was out on the road to Fort Frederica,
and when I got to the stables, I saw that Mrs. Commodore had forgotten to leave the light burning
above the door to the barn. I fumbled in the dark for
my key. Inside, the air was close and warm and filled
with the smell of resting animals. Trader nuzzled at
the bars above his feed bowl, and I reached in and
patted his neck. He shook his head appreciatively. He
had shed a tooth since that afternoon.

"You can come in," I said over my shoulder to
Fernando.

He stepped soundlessly into the circle of light.

"This is Trader. He's my favorite," I said. "The
others are Alfred and Sassy, Roscoe, Caesar, and
China Doll. The ponies are at the end."

While I walked the length of the barn, eyeballing
the horses, Fernando got acquainted with each of

them in turn. It occurred to me that he must know something about animals. He didn't seem a bit awkward or ill at ease. Maybe that's why he had come to the stables at dawn that first morning. Maybe it was to see the horses instead of me.

I don't know what got into me, but I decided to strip Trader's stall to the ground, even though it'd only been a day since Rob Allard had done it last. "Horse people are crazy people," Mrs. Commodore was fond of telling me. "It's like a terminal disease." Maybe I was really becoming a horse person.

Or maybe I was just still mad at Dad for insisting that Fernando come with me to take care of the horses. It had been my idea to go ahead and have him and Rea over. I guess I felt sorry for him. I'd been looking forward all day to being at the stables without Rob Allard or even Mrs. Commodore around. But I also figured that maybe Dad wanted to be alone for a minute with Rea. And Fernando intrigued me. I can't deny that.

"It's going to take some time," I said to him, "so just do whatever you want. I'd be kind of careful with Alfred, though. Sometimes he bites. There's a chair in Mrs. Commodore's office, if you want to sit down and wait."

I led Trader to an empty stall at the end and told him I'd be back to get him. Then I found the wheelbarrow and shovel and set to work.

I don't know how long it took me; in fact, I gradually lost track of time altogether. The rhythm I had settled into was hypnotic: shoveling till the wheelbarrow was full, rolling it out into the cold air beneath all those stars, emptying it, and coming back for more. Normally work like that clears my head. But I couldn't get El Paraíso off my mind. I'd finally found a detailed map of El Salvador in a *Newsweek* article about the war. I'd only skimmed the article, but I had stared at that map for what seemed like hours, memorizing the names of the thirteen provinces and the major towns. The provinces had musical names, like Ahuachapán and San Vicente, and this map was the first concrete proof I'd had that there was really a place called El Paraíso after all. It was in a province called Chalatenango, which sounded like a dance. I wondered what kind of dance they danced in Chalatenango province on Christmas Eve. I imagined these long embroidered skirts, pleated and with bright borders, and the women holding them out while the men danced around them in straw hats and scarves. But right in the middle of my imaginary dance floor, as in the middle of all my Christmases, stood Dad.

"It's rough for drunks around Christmas," he had said before Rea and Fernando got there that night. Right, I thought at the time, but not nearly as bad as it is on their kids.

I knew I should have been content. Dad was sober, after all. The Christmas tree was blinking in the corner. Dad and I opened one present each. It was a family tradition of ours, to open just one present on Christmas Eve. Maybe it was the tradition that reminded me of all the Christmases Dad's drinking had ruined.

There was the year it snowed on Christmas morning, the first and only time in anybody's memory in Atlanta, but by the time I finally got Dad out of bed to take me out in it (he stayed in the bathroom almost an hour and he was so hungover he put his shoes on the wrong feet), the snow had melted and all the other kids had gone back in. That was the night he got in a fistfight with Mother's brother Derrick, who lives in Germany now. They were arguing over the pronunciation of the word *umbilicus*. Then there were the toys left unassembled, the batteries that never got bought. One Christmas Eve, I woke up thinking I had heard Santa Claus. It was Dad pissing in the hall closet. But that was not the worst. The worst was when he invited a couple he'd met at the Ramada Inn lounge to Christmas at our house. They'd lost their mobile home in a fire. The adults spent the whole morning arguing in the kitchen, where the cigarette smoke was so thick you'd asphyxiate just walking through.

"What's wrong, April?" Dad said. "Are you all right?"

"Yeah," I lied. It was at just that moment that Rea and Fernando had knocked at the door. I didn't know whether I was glad to see them or not. That was my problem, I decided. I didn't know how to feel about things.

And all the work I was doing stripping Trader's stall hadn't clarified matters a bit. After I had spread the fresh wood shavings, I brought Trader back to show him how nice I'd made everything for him. I'd already groomed him that afternoon, but now I did the really special things. Instead of just brushing him down, I went over him with a currycomb, using wide, circular motions, and then I cleaned his nostrils and under his tail. After combing his mane, I picked his tail one hair at a time and plaited it into a gorgeous, long braid. Then I picked his hooves, clipped his muzzle, and checked his legs for splints. It wasn't necessary to wrap his legs, but I did it anyway, exactly as Mrs. Commodore had taught me.

Standing back, I admired my work. Trader's chestnut coat was lustrous, his eyes rake-hell and alert. Finally my anger had lifted. Then I heard the sound of a horse whinnying from the tack room. I suddenly remembered Fernando and wondered what on earth he had been doing all this time.

When I entered the room, I saw. Fernando had cleaned up the place and had gotten Alfred completely tacked; he was just now tightening the girth.

"What do you think you're doing?" I asked.

"Getting the horse ready."

"For what?"

"To ride."

"Wait just a cotton-picking minute. You can't do that."

"I have some money," he said.

"That's not the point."

He mounted him. Right in front of my eyes. Just as smooth as you can imagine, like he'd been riding all his life. "What is the point?" he asked.

"The stable's closed," I said. "It's Christmas Eve.

You haven't signed the release forms. Our insurance wouldn't cover it if anything happened." And the more things I thought of to say, the funnier it started sounding to me. Fernando was smiling, too, the first time I think I'd ever seen him smile, and I remembered what Dad had said about him not knowing the meaning of pleasure.

"All right," I said, "but I'm telling you, you just wait till I get Trader saddled before you leave this barn, and when I say we come back in, I mean it."

"*A sus órdenes,*" he said, which means something like at your service.

This is crazy, I was thinking to myself. Absolutely insane. But I felt like I had all the time in the world and nothing really to lose.

The beach at night in the dead of winter, even without a moon, is something to see. The line where the water lapped on the sand still held some light, but the ocean itself was as dark as a pit. The only electric lights were from a hotel, a couple of the beach houses, and the swinging eye of the lighthouse way over at the village. I knew I was breaking all kinds of rules and that Mrs. Commodore and Dad would be disappointed and probably very pissed if they found out. But I'd obeyed the rules all my life, and there wasn't much to show for it.

Fernando broke Alfred into a gallop. I couldn't believe my eyes: Alfred! And turned him on a dime and galloped back through the water, splashing me, but I didn't care. Alfred hadn't gone that fast since the day the lightning almost barbecued the boy from Atlanta.

"He's a good horse," Fernando said, "but maybe too well fed."

"Where'd you learn to ride?" I asked. We were side by side now, headed for the point near the rock jetties, where you can see the lighthouse well.

"With the people's army," he said.

"Oh," I said. I didn't know what the people's army was. "You were in the cavalry, huh?"

Fernando shook his head. "We used the horses to carry supplies. In the countryside where there aren't any roads."

I wanted to say, "Was this in Chalatenango province?" but instead I said, "I'd never been on a horse until this September. Can you believe that? I just talked myself into the job. You like your job okay?"

"I like flowers," he said.

"Dad told me you had family in California."

"A sister."

"Younger or older?"

"She is maybe your age."

"Have you thought about going to see her?"

"No." He flicked his reins and Alfred went tearing off again. The spray hit me in the face this time. Fernando rode high in the saddle. He must have felt incredibly light to Alfred. He was not like a normal American boy his age. He hardly had any substance. His bones must have been hollow, like a bird's. I watched them disappear into the dark, but I could

54

follow their progress along the beach by the sound of the hooves through the water, like cracking ice.

When they reemerged from the dark, Fernando's head was low, his cheek flush against Alfred's neck. It was so dark on this stretch that if I hadn't known who Fernando was, I wouldn't have been able to recognize him. He lifted his head, and there was a look of such intensity there, it almost frightened me.

He wheeled Alfred around so we were side by side again. "What were you thinking just then?" I asked. He didn't answer me. Maybe he hadn't heard me, but I didn't repeat the question. Maybe I didn't want to know the answer.

"Mrs. Commodore would kill me if she knew what we were doing," I said. His unsettled look made me clarify: "Not actually kill me. That's a figure of speech. It means she'd be very unhappy."

"We have figures of speech, too," he said, but he said it as though he meant something else.

The rocks came upon us quicker than I had expected. The horses moved more gingerly there. After the jetty, the beach picked up again, but we wouldn't be going that far. We could see from the scattered lights the way the beach curved toward the village. We stopped and waited. The air was cold. The town was utterly quiet.

Out over the water we could see the beam from the lighthouse make its way past Jekyll Island and out to sea. From somewhere out there came the clang of a buoy, a comforting sound, but tinged with loneliness. I took a deep breath filled with salt spray and the smell of horses. The beam from the lighthouse was swinging around. It was touching the crests of the little waves and the spit of sand at the head of the sound and then the jetty and the beach itself. It began racing up the sand toward us. I looked at Fernando. He was looking at me. The light suddenly burst on our faces. I saw things I'd never seen before, the curve of his lip, the ragged part of his hair, the shadow of his long eyelashes, as delicate as a girl's. The scar down the side of his neck stood out like a relief map. I felt like I wanted to touch it. His eyes themselves were lit with something I couldn't name. It was like sorrow, and not like sorrow, a kind of nakedness. I got this crazy feeling that he knew exactly what I had been going through, that he was going through the same things himself. I might as well have been looking into my own face, and I think this was when I knew I was going to fall into something like love with him.

8

(Falling in love was my second mistake. I have never liked the way love makes me feel. Suddenly you can't follow conversations, you make turns onto one-way streets, you forget what you're in the store to buy. The worst is at night when you can't keep your thoughts straight and the guy's face tumbles around in your brain until you can't even remember what he looks like anymore. It's as though you wouldn't be able to recognize him on the street. Then a single detail, like a tilted eyebrow or the shape of his chin—in Fernando's case it was his scar, which led like a road to the line of his jaw—suddenly makes his whole face come into focus again. For that instant it's like a face I know I'll never forget.

On Christmas Eve I thought I'd never get to sleep, but I must have slept some that night, because I woke up when Dad said, "Merry Christmas." It was still dark. I couldn't make out Dad's face, but I could smell him—a mingling of sleep, coffee, and shaving cream. He turned on my table lamp, and I squinted. He was fully dressed in jeans, boots, and his old Georgia Tech sweatshirt with the stinging bees.

"Have you lost your mind?" I said.

"Where's your Christmas spirit?"

"It must be four o'clock in the morning."

"Five-fifteen," he said. "Come on. We've got to hurry."

My stomach turned. He was drunk. The thought had a horrible familiarity to it, terrifying and exhilarating, like the beginning of an amusement park ride. I could see it all before me, being jerked out of bed in the dark on Christmas morning. Who knew what was going on somewhere else in the house? Who knew what I'd have to go through that day? He pulled the curtains back, but no light came in. The night outside the window was a wet slab of black. There hadn't been a moon. "Why are you doing this to me?" I asked. But when he turned back around, I saw that he wasn't drunk after all. Just crazy. I pulled the covers over my head.

"Come on, April, look alive," he said.

"Go away."

"Santa left something for you."

"It can wait."

"No it can't." He must have sat on the bed, because I could feel the springs give.

I lowered the covers. "What is it?"

"Bundle up," he said. "I'm gonna teach you how to drive a straight shift."

I saw it first from the kitchen window when Dad turned on the outside light, a glimmer of red under the trees. "Steady as you go," he said, steering me by the shoulders out the back door. I was holding both cups of coffee, and I knew the minute I stepped out into the air that I should have put on a sweater under my windbreaker. I was freezing, but I don't know whether it was the cold that made me shiver or the sight of the Jeep in front of the garage.

"It's an old one, but the engine's in good shape. I hope you like the color."

"Gosh, it's beautiful," I said. "You mean it's really mine?"

"It's a matter of necessity. We *have* to have two cars now."

I looked up at him. He hadn't stepped off the porch stoop, and he was shifting his weight back and forth like he does when he's embarrassed or ill at ease. I stepped up and gave him a quick hug. "Thanks, Dad." I didn't know what else to say. The Jeep was a dream, but I was scared of it. I saw myself stalling on a hill and the brakes giving way and the Jeep rolling backward through intersections and houses.

He must have been reading my mind. "If you can learn to ride a horse, you can learn to drive a straight shift," he said.

We drove out to the turnoff to Christ's Church and Fort Frederica, Dad behind the wheel, and then we changed places. He hadn't been kidding about the Jeep being old. The odometer had already started over at least once, and the dashboard was split from the sun. It had a top, he said, but he couldn't figure out how to get it snapped on right, so we'd have to just brace ourselves against the cold. He was vague about where he'd gotten it, which led me to believe that maybe a patient had talked him into taking it off his hands. The paint job was sloppy in places, and the glove compartment popped open whenever we hit a bump in the road, but all these things just made it more special, of course. I'd never had a car, didn't think I'd ever have one until I was on my own. Dad believed in saving up for things, although *he* never had. Even now, he reminded me that I'd be responsible for the insurance premiums and tags and gas and maintenance. "Let me learn how to drive it first," I said.

He showed me the throttle, which he said I'd have to leave out about a quarter of an inch even after the engine got going good, and he ran me through the gears, over and over, while we sat on the shoulder of the road with the engine off and the parking lights on. He said the clutch was a little tight, but that was better than being too loose, and that I'd get used to it.

"It's like learning to ride a bike," he said. "Once you get the feel of it, you never forget."

Even though it was nowhere near sunrise, there were cars on the road. Their headlights played across Dad's face, bands of light and dark.

"You want to give it a try?" he asked.

I nodded, but because of the other cars, he decided to go farther up the road toward Hamilton

Point. On the way, he thanked me for taking Fernando to the stables. "I don't think he has any friends here," he said.

I tried to keep my voice steady, nonchalant. "I don't know why. He's really a pretty nice guy."

"That's what I thought, too. Not like most North American kids, present company excepted of course."

"I know what you mean."

"It's a shame he's got a banged-up heart."

The words stung, like he'd insulted me.

"He doesn't look sick to me," I said.

I could feel Dad's eyes on me in the dark.

"No reason he can't live a normal life," he admitted. "He just needs to watch it is all."

Dad took the curve by the big sand pit and jammed the stick into third. It popped back out. "You'll have to watch that," he said, easing it back in.

"I've always had a lot of faith in the government," he continued. "I guess it's because I came of age during the civil rights movement, when the feds were on the right side of things. But the more I find out about immigration policy, the more I begin to think we've got some screwballs in Washington who are out to make life miserable for people to no good end. People fleeing political repression in their own countries, for instance. They get here, and what do we do? We arrest them, deport them, and pretend we don't know what's going to happen to them when they return home."

"What *does* happen to them?"

61

"It depends. Some of them wind up in prison. Some of them just disappear. The point is, we used to be a country that took oppressed people in. Maybe those days are over." He glanced in the rearview mirror. "This looks like a good spot."

He stopped in the middle of the road with the engine in neutral and changed places with me. I held the trembling gearshift ball in my hand and felt for the clutch pedal with my foot.

"The trick," he said, "is to give it enough gas so that it doesn't die on you, but not so much that the engine jerks when the clutch engages. Think of it as one smooth continuous arc."

Right. I simultaneously gave the accelerator gas and eased up on the clutch. "You got it," he said. It had been pure luck. The Jeep was moving, and I shifted into second. "All right!"

I was too flushed with success to notice the cold wind whipping through the Jeep's interior.

"You might want to try third now," Dad said.

"What?"

"Try shifting into third!" The reason I hadn't heard him was that the engine was revving so high. I stomped the clutch and tried to force the stick into third. It wouldn't go. I panicked. My foot came off the clutch, and when I tried to push the stick into third again, the gears ground. I slammed on the brake. The engine shuddered to a stop, and the head-lights shot an eerie glow across the asphalt and into a stand of spider-thin pine.

"Did I ruin it?"

"No, no. Everything's fine. That third gear is tricky," he said. He ran through the gears again while I handled the clutch. "I think you just have to lay it in there. You know what I mean?"

"Lay it in there?"

"Kind of deliver it. Don't force it. Lead it. Let it take itself in."

I cranked the engine, but didn't give it enough gas going into first so it died.

"That's all right," he said. "You know, you can probably just start it in second on level ground like this."

I tried again. It died again. "I guess I lost the hang of it," I said.

"Third time's a charm."

He was right. Suddenly we were coasting past fields of marsh grass and cabbage palms. I held my breath and eased it toward third. It fell in, like a key in its tumblers.

"Great!" he said. "You're cooking now."

I gave it some more gas. The cold air whipped at the elbows of my windbreaker. My hands felt hard and raw.

"Kid's got a lot of promise," Dad said over the wind.

"I can't hear you," I said.

"I'm talking about Fernando."

"Oh, yeah," I said, too loud. I was braking for a white cow that was crossing the road. It looked straight at me and shuffled backward off the road like an aging boxer. No telling where we were now.

"Take it to the point," Dad said, "and then let's go back to the old Coast Guard headquarters. In thirty minutes the sun's gonna rise over the ocean. You haven't seen that yet, have you?"

"No."

"That's the real reason I got you up this early," he smiled. For a minute there I started to believe he had always been this good to me.

"The reason why we have to have two cars now is simple," he said. He had put his arm around my shoulder as we walked down the sandy path to the beach. "The hospital in Brunswick's going to let me handle some cases there on a trial basis starting the first of the year."

"That's great," I said, and then the significance of it hit me. When the hospital let him practice there, his career would be back on track. "I mean, that's just super. When'd you find out?"

"Last week. I should have told you then, but I didn't want to tip my hand about the Jeep." He said he wouldn't be able to see his own patients at the hospital and he couldn't perform any invasive diagnostic procedures. Even routine examinations would be monitored for a while. He'd be largely confined to taking medical histories and making rounds for other doctors whose patients were about to be released anyway. But still it was a big deal.

We were dropping off the dunes past the wax myrtle and prickly pears. Behind us the abandoned Coast Guard station gleamed ivory against the overcast sky. Because of the clouds, we wouldn't be able to see the sun come up directly out of the ocean, but Dad hid his disappointment about that. We wound up just walking along the beach while the air turned gray around us. "There's something else," he said. "I've been needing to do this for a long time, but I haven't been able to find the words." Like idiots, we had taken off our shoes; the water was frigid. "A.A.'s a twelve-step program, you know." I'd heard of that. "One of the steps we have to take is to make amends to all the people we hurt when we were drinking." He glanced at me. "So I'm sorry, April. I hope you can forgive me some day."

He was sorry. Huh. We kept on walking. I tried to think of something to say, but I just couldn't come up with anything. He'd stolen my childhood, and I don't think he realized that. Even if he had realized it, saying he was sorry wouldn't have brought those years back. I didn't say a thing and hoped my silence wouldn't be taken as a sign that I had forgiven him, because I hadn't and I thought I never would.

The lights on Jekyll Island grew dimmer and finally went out. The sea gulls started wheeling above our heads. Somewhere behind the bank of clouds, the sun was probably rising now. We stopped and stood beside one another, staring out to sea. The surf was dark and rank with seaweed. Suddenly a slit appeared in the clouds. It widened from a thin golden line into a wedge of sun.

Dad stretched out his arms. The wind was in his hair, what hair he had left. He had been a killer kind of handsome when he was twenty, I could see that from his photos, and even now he had a kind of presence that not all big men, simply because they're big, have. The clouds closed up again. Dad dropped his arms and stuffed his thick hands into the pockets of his jeans. Maybe he was thinking about his future. For the first time in years he actually had one. For some reason I can't explain, that thought depressed me no end.

9

Things got better after Christmas. I had put the stuff about Fernando into perspective. This was not love, I told myself, but the kind of feeling you have for stray animals and your friends' younger brothers.

The Wednesday before school started back, Rea Britt called to ask me to lunch the next day at the Sea Island resort. It was the first time an adult who was not a relative had ever invited me to lunch. I said sure, even though I'd have to get Rob Allard to cover for me in the ring. He'd been more of a jerk than usual lately. He said he'd driven by the stables on Christmas Eve and had seen that I'd taken two of the horses out for a ride on the beach. He had half a mind to tell Mrs. Commodore about it. I said go right ahead. I was playing on the special relationship he knew Mrs. Commodore and I had, but actually I was a little worried.

When I hung up with Rea, I started planning what to wear. The fact that I wondered only fleetingly whether Fernando would be working that day was proof that the ride on the beach on Christmas Eve had been an aberration. Rea probably understood such things. I figured she'd been in love a million times, but had always managed, like me, to convince herself it was only her imagination working overtime.

Rea was standing by the bird cages in the lobby of the resort when I got there. She had on straw flats and a white cotton dress with seashells embroidered into the neckline. I had overdone it again: a lime-colored blazer, pleated trousers, fake pearls, and a hideous pair of my mother's navy high heels. Oh well. Nobody had ever accused me of good taste.

"You look stunning," she said.

I must have turned a dozen shades of red, because she patted my arm before steering me down the hall past mirrors in gilt frames, Audubon prints, and banana trees in planters the size of bathtubs. In every one of the mirrors, I looked like an overripe fruit.

"Forgive me for not showing you around," she said, "but I don't want to run into my boss. He's been on my case about Fernando today. Apparently he thinks the resort could get into some kind of legal trouble. I told him to direct all questions to me. Public relations is my job, after all. I can put a good face on anything."

"Why's everybody making such a big deal about Fernando?"

"Maybe they don't have anything better to do," she said. She was a good head taller than me. I thought she was going to have to duck when we went under the archway into the dining room, but she didn't.

"Good grief," I said and stopped in my tracks. I'd never seen the dining room of the resort before. It was something out of the Arabian Nights. The pillars and arches continued on down the main aisle toward a mirrored wall in back that extended the illusion of an endless promenade. The wallpaper was a tropical jungle scene, with orchids climbing the walls. Some gauzy kinds of curtains billowed in an artificial breeze. The chandeliers were shaped like Russian Easter eggs, and each table had long white candles set in overturned gold tortoise shells.

"Don't let the veneer of elegance fool you," she said. "This is still a place for people to vacation at, although my idea of a vacation is a splintery cabin across the highway from the beach. Where did your family go on vacations?"

"Florida." I left it at that.

We were waiting to be shown to our table. Rea smiled at me, a cautious, tight-lipped smile. It occurred to me that she might be nervous, but I couldn't guess why. A smooth operator in a white sport coat showed us to our table, where Rea insisted I take the view of the marina and the flagstone path that led to a miniature beach. The waiter hadn't even asked Rea for her drink order. He simply brought a bottle of chilled Perrier and poured it over crushed ice in a long-stemmed glass and then garnished it with a twist of lime.

"Thank you, Paul," she said.

"And you, Miss?"

"Just water," I said. "And a Coke." Just saying the word relaxed me. I took off my blazer and hung it on the back of my chair. That felt better. The peach blouse wasn't as dressy as it looked. I'd worn it with jeans to the village a million times. There was even a raspberry yogurt stain on the right sleeve, but it didn't show.

"So, you're looking forward to school starting back?"

"You bet."

"And you like the Jeep well enough, but you really wish that Jack had gotten you a horse."

"Did he tell you that?"

"No. I'm kidding."

"I *love* the Jeep."

The waiter brought my Coke. I unfolded my napkin and spread it in my lap.

"I'd like to go for a ride in it sometime," Rea said.

"I don't know. You might want to give me a few weeks. I just about ran into a telephone pole by the airport while I was downshifting yesterday."

Rea smiled and glanced away. She had already ordered, but I was having trouble making up my mind. I finally decided on a grouper steak. Past the marina, a shower was moving slowly toward the horizon. Below it the water was dappled and gray. Otherwise, the sun was out, and the air had that February feel to it, high clouds and a sharp-edged breeze, even though it was only the first week of January and winter was nowhere near over yet.

"I've never asked you why you left Atlanta," Rea said. "Is that an okay question?"

"Sure," I said. "It's too big. Too Yankeefied." Then I bit my lip, unreasonably afraid Rea might be a Yankee.

"I know what you mean," she said, and I knew I was safe. "But you get along all right with your mother, don't you?"

I shrugged. We never had fights, if that's what she meant.

"Well it was good of you to come be with Jack at this time in his life. He says you're taking awfully good care of him."

I'm embarrassed by praise, but I wanted to hear more about this.

"It's a different life, isn't it?" she asked instead.

"What do you mean?"

"Living with a sober man."

I nodded. "What did you call those things you ordered?"

"Papillotes. They're like puffy envelopes with snapper inside. You can try one if they ever come. The service is impeccable here, but not very brisk."

"Were you really a drunk?" I asked her.

71

"I *am* a drunk," she said. "I just don't drink any-more."

"Oh, yeah." That A.A. talk drove me crazy sometimes. "But you weren't like Dad."

"I wasn't?"

"You couldn't have been."

"Why not?" Her eyelids crinkled. Was she amused at my expense?

"Oh, nothing."

"No, seriously." She leaned back in her chair. "Tell me what you mean."

"Dad was a slob. You know, his shirts all had cigarette burns in them and nothing he wore ever matched."

She smiled.

"His car, it was like a burgundy Oldsmobile with fake leather seats, there were *things* growing in it. And the ashtray was always full. He had go cups in the floorboard. People's medical records were spilling off the backseat. One time when he double-parked and the police towed his car away—his driver's license had been jerked and he was afraid to go to the city garage and claim the car—he was so paranoid he thought they'd arrest him on the spot so he hired a cab driver to go down there and find his Oldsmobile and hunt through the stuff in the backseat for a patient's chest X ray."

Rea covered her smile with her hand. "I'm not laughing *at* him," she said.

"I don't care. It is funny, I guess. At the time, it was just weird. I remember thinking maybe he had brain damage, his memory was so bad. He'd even forget my name when he was trying to introduce me to people. Other times I just figured we weren't that important to him, that maybe nobody was."

"You've told him this?"

"Are you kidding?"

"No."

Our salads arrived, and I realized I'd been talking my head off. "Well, so that's the way things were," I said. "He was nothing like you."

Rea was silent for a minute. She was buttering her bread slowly, thoughtfully. "I don't know what you see when you look at me, April," she finally said, "but I'm just an ordinary drunk like your dad."

"Right."

"I never had a husband or child to inflict myself on, but there were plenty of other people, people who were important to me at the time."

We ate in silence. "My mother died before I dried out, for instance," she continued.

I don't like hearing about dead people.

"I had boyfriends, too, most of them imminently forgettable, but one or two were interesting enough that I'd think, hey, wait a minute, but nothing ever came of them. I got pregnant once. Twice, actually." She ducked her head, as if to concentrate on the huge wedge of tomato she was carving into bite-size bits.

I did *not* want to hear this.

"I had abortions both times," she said. "I knew who the father of the last one was. The child would have been about your age by now."

Okay, I get the point, I thought.

"I don't mean to ruin your meal."

Go right ahead, I wanted to say. I'm used to ruined meals. I'm Mad Jack Hunter's daughter, remember?

"Why aren't you in a support group, April?" she asked.

Outside, the sun had gone in. The entire sky had changed. It looked curdled. Buttermilk sky. Is this what they call it?

"I think you'd enjoy it."

"When you met Dad," I said, "did he tell you I had a twin sister?"

She looked startled, exactly what I had intended. Of course he hadn't told her.

"She came after me, stillborn. Mother wanted to name her May."

"How unusual," Rea said. "Not the name."

"Well, I think it's pretty weird. April, May. Like characters in a nursery rhyme."

"It must have been a terrible blow. No wonder you're so special to your parents."

I shrugged.

"A twin sister," she repeated. She dabbed her mouth with the corner of her napkin. They were taking our salad bowls away, refilling our glasses, and bringing in the sizzling seafood on plates.

"Don't ever mention that to Dad."

"I wouldn't," she said. "But why?"

"I would just rather you didn't." I neglected to tell her the entire thing was a lie, made up whole cloth on the spot. I felt pretty clever about the name, May, but I was astonished at myself. It was like a kind of madness that had come over me.

I was standing just outside the archway to the dining room when I saw Fernando making his way down the hall. He was dressed in a dark green jumpsuit and a pair of run-over, off-brand sneakers. He carried a water bucket with the resort's emblem on the side, and he was stopping to water the plants along the way, the banana trees and potted avocados and all the hanging ferns and wandering Jew. I didn't think he had seen me yet. At one of the bird cages he paused to tap the feeder and make a delicate whistling sound. The birds, a pair of iridescent finches, hopped from bar to bar.

Fernando stepped back when a middle-aged couple on their way from the dining room started making over the birds. I mean, he literally disappeared into the wallpaper until they moved on, and then he continued watering the plants. Another pair of diners passed by without noticing him. He was on tiptoe in front of a window, picking the brown leaves off a maidenhair fern.

When he turned around, I could tell that he had seen me long before. His eyes were already composed to meet mine.

"*Hola*," he said.

"Hi."

He came to my side of the hall, where there was a window box of begonia that maybe needed watering.

He tilted the can, and we both watched the water soak into the loam. I was struck all over again by how slight he was, how insignificant. It had been ridiculous for me to imagine myself in love with him.

But when he looked up at me again, I started getting vertigo. It was like I was on a train pulling away from the station and I couldn't tell what was moving, the train or the platform. "Miss Britt told me you were going to have lunch with her," he said. "Did you enjoy it?"

"The food was great."

"I know the cooks," he said.

In the mirror across the hall I could see Rea coming toward us from behind. I swear she slowed down when she saw us. She was strolling, her head cocked at a solicitous angle. Fernando had not seen her. I know he hadn't or he wouldn't have done what he did next. He reached out and tucked a stray strand of hair behind my ear. His touch was as light as a butterfly's.

"Fernando is very mysterious to me," Rea said. She'd insisted on walking me to the Jeep, and we'd paused at the wooden fence by the marina to watch a sailboat with an enormous mast make its berth. "He's shy almost to the point of vanishing. It's like the upstairs of my house is less than empty when he's there. I've never seen him eat."

"You don't eat together?"

"I cook for him, but he always takes this tiny portion and goes upstairs with it. What he leaves on the plate often looks like it's more than what was there in the first place."

"Maybe he doesn't feel well," I said.

"Maybe so, or maybe it's a cultural thing. He acts like he works for *me,* not the resort, and as domestic help shouldn't eat in the same room. I've tried to straighten him out about all this, but it seems to embarrass him."

"Huh," I said.

"And he never initiates a conversation. He listens well, is in fact the most wonderful listener I've ever known, but he never volunteers an opinion about anything, except the other week, after we'd seen you on Christmas Eve, when he said something about you, something very nice, I thought."

My antennae went bananas.

"He said you had an inner light."

I continued to hold her gaze, although my impulse was to glance away.

"I think he's very perceptive, April. I'm not as organized in my thinking, but I've been feeling that way about you, too."

Our hands met on the fence rail. It was a totally unselfconscious gesture. I really liked Rea, and I felt like she liked me back apart from her friendship with Dad.

"And to think there were once *two* of you," she said, giving my hand a playful shake.

10

I don't know what got into me that night after I finished up at the stables. Dad had already left for his A.A. meeting when I got home. He'd left a note on the counter saying he'd had to buy an answering machine and a beeper. His few patients on the island were calling like crazy now that they knew he was going into the hospital in Brunswick some. It's not unfair to say that people do better when they know their doctor's available than they do when he's busy or out of town.

"I never seem to get things right when I try to talk to you," he continued in the note. I figured he was still going over his apology on the beach.

"Don't be silly," I wrote on the bottom. "If I'm not here when you get in, I'm at the village. Back soon." I thought about "Love, April" but signed it instead "A."

The village, my foot. I drove straight to Rea's

house on Old Demere Trace and parked out front. It had turned into a heavy, warm night. The temperature had risen after sunset instead of falling. We were in for peculiar weather, and I regretted not having figured out yet how to get the Jeep top on.

It is possible to park directly in front of someone's house on St. Simons without attracting undue attention. I guess it's because of the live oaks, which make everything, even cars, seem insignificant, and the fact that it's a resort island, and strangers are always leaving their cars, mostly with out-of-state tags, in unusual places. Bird watchers sometimes wander into your yard from the marshes and strike up a conversation, as though you'd invited them over for tea.

I waited under the live oaks, my heart thumping. A streetlight threw the shadows of a crape myrtle across the walkway and onto the porch steps. One light was on in Rea's living room. Her house is not old enough to be quaint and not new enough to be stylish. It's kind of nondescript, an off-white frame bungalow with azalea bushes out front and a second-story bedroom clearly added on in back. This bedroom had its own outside entrance, at the top of a steep flight of stairs. That's where her mother had lived, and now Fernando lived there.

One of these days, I thought, I am going to look back on this and be real embarrassed. It would have been different if I could have gotten up enough nerve to walk up and knock on the door, but to just sit out front with my palms getting sweaty, watching the rearview mirror afraid somebody might see me there

—that was just too juvenile for words. I had it in my head that Fernando was up there emptying the pockets of his jumpsuit after work. Why that image, I do not know. He hears Rea calling him to dinner. He looks up. He tries to figure out how to get down the stairs unseen, to put something on his plate and get back upstairs before she can see him.

I looked in the rearview mirror and thought what a sicko I was. That's when I saw his hand on the door. He was leaning into the Jeep, his face still in darkness.

"You scared me," I said.

"Is anything wrong?"

"No. I'm just out for a drive." I had my hands on the wheel, like I was going forty miles an hour and he had just happened to jump aboard.

"Would you like to come in?" he asked.

I glanced at the house. "Rea's not expecting me," I said.

"She is not here," he said, and his face emerged from the darkness. His hair was still wet, he must have just showered, and he had on one of those faded Surf's Up shirts that used to be popular but which nobody my age would be caught dead in anymore. On him, it looked a little sad, but right.

"I'd better not," I said without thinking. It was the knee-jerk good girl thing to say. My Atlanta tuba player would have wheedled me out of it, but Fernando just nodded.

"Do you want to take a walk?" he asked.

"I've got a better idea," I said. "You haven't ridden in my Jeep, have you?"

He shook his head. Of course he hadn't.

"Hop in. I'll show you the sights."

"Hop in?"

"It's a figure of speech. It means open the door and have a seat."

I forgot to pull the choke out, so the engine wouldn't crank at first, but Fernando fiddled with the knobs on the dash until he found the right one, the engine caught with a *whumpf,* and soon we were cruising under the oaks on Demere Retreat Trace and onto the road toward the causeway and Brunswick, the port city across the sound. It was pure chance which way we were headed. I was too nervous to know what I was doing. It was like I was in a trance.

I loved the Jeep, but I didn't have any illusions about it. Sure, it was special to me, but I knew it was really just an old heap. Rob Allard hadn't even said anything about it when he saw me pull up in it at the stables, not that anything Rob Allard says ever matters to me. It gets you where you're going, but nobody's going to go out of their way to tell you how cool you are for owning one.

For Fernando, though, it was different. He ran his hands over the split dashboard, peered into the glove compartment, settled himself in the seat. He took out his comb and ran it through his hair, using the outside mirror on the passenger side, even though the wind whipped his hair all crazy again as soon as the light turned green. I had known he would like it. That's another thing about love. You start seeing everything through the guy's eyes, a special place on the sand between two elder bushes, a movie you know he'd like, a book he'll never read. I could never explain to Dad, of course, but the first thing I thought when I saw the Jeep under the trees on Christmas morning was how much Fernando would like it, the theory being that he had probably never had anything.

You see, we hadn't been riding for ten minutes, hadn't said a word yet, but I was starting to want Fernando in the same way I knew he'd want the Jeep. I was having all kinds of thoughts, that maybe because they were such devout Catholics in El Salvador, the girls were all virtuous and uptight. This was probably the first time he'd been with a girl unchaperoned, and an Anglo girl at that, a Methodist with blond hair. I was stretching it there, but my hair *is* almost honey-colored in the right kind of light. So it was probably a good idea we were heading toward the causeway and Brunswick, because that's where the lights were. The more light the better, an antidote to what I was working myself into. I gunned the engine to pass a pair of snowbirds in a Winnebago with Pigeon Forge decals on the back, and out there on the causeway above the Marshes of Glynn and the four rivers cutting black and silent through the silver grass, I turned to look at him.

He grinned shyly at me. It was shocking. Fernando was just a kid. I couldn't be desiring him, I told myself. It was a preposterous state of affairs.

"Where are we going?" he asked.

"There's a Huddle House in Brunswick that's got hot apple pie with cheese. Ever had any?"

He shook his head.

"You'll like it. It's very American. You can get ice cream on the top and so forth. I could use a Diet Coke. Does my driving make you nervous?"

"No. I like the breeze."

But under the high fluorescent lights of the Huddle House, Fernando started looking older to me, and I began having all kinds of thoughts again. Desire is so unpredictable. And irrational. I always seem to want the wrong people and the wrong things.

"The bus station is right around the corner," he said, as if I had asked.

"You came here on a bus?" I said. I had pictured him washing ashore in a bright orange lifeboat.

"Yes. I caught it in Texas, in Brownsville, and rode for two days straight."

Why this made me jealous, I can't explain.

"I had the clothes I was wearing. That's all."

The waitress brought our pie, my Coke, and his glass of milk. She gave him the once over, and I realized I'd made a minor mistake. Brunswick didn't have much use for local girls hanging out with dark-skinned men.

"You've seen some territory," I said. It was not a question, but he took it as one.

"You cannot see much out of a box car," he said.

"I thought you came by bus."

"From Brownsville. I came from Mexico by train."

Something in that jarred an image from television: heat, boxcars, the refugee problem. Some kind of awful tragedy.

"My uncle Will in Atlanta says Mexico is flat as a tabletop," I said. I don't have an uncle named Will.

"Some places maybe. We went up and down mountains for days."

He had taken one bite of his pie and set the fork down, just like Dad. It must be a thing with men.

"Why did you come here, Fernando?" I asked.

He glanced at the waitress, who was hovering around with a pinched expression on her face, like she'd gotten a whiff of something unpleasant. I knew for sure I'd made a mistake.

"When I got to Houston, I just traveled east," he said.

"I don't mean why you came to St. Simons. I mean, why did you come to the states?"

He smiled. "Your father has been to El Salvador. Has he ever told you what it is like?"

"He says it's very beautiful."

"Yes. But there is a war there."

"I know that."

"They would have killed me if I had stayed." Now he did pick up his fork, and he ate the rest of his pie methodically, bite by bite. A line of traffic was streaming by outside the window, probably from a high school basketball game. I knew what any other

84

person would have said: You must have seen some terrible things. But I couldn't say that.

"Why didn't you just head for Los Angeles?" I asked instead. "Don't you have a sister there?"

He finished chewing and wiped his mouth with his napkin. "Her husband was a member of the Treasury Police."

I could tell this was supposed to mean something to me, but it didn't, and he knew he'd have to explain.

"The Treasury Police are part of the military. And the military has been fighting the guerrillas for many years. In my town, you're either on one side or the other. There is no in-between. Either you're a guerrilla, or you're a government informer. I wasn't really a guerrilla, but I could not give the police the information they wanted, so I had to leave."

"You said you learned to ride horses in the mountains."

He lowered his voice even further and leaned across the table. "I had to run supplies for the guerrillas for a while, to get safe passage through the mountains to Honduras. I was a *mensajero*, a messenger."

"Then what?"

"There were refugee camps in Honduras, where I could hide and make plans. After a couple of months, I left with some others in the back of a banana truck through Guatemala into Mexico, where we sneaked onto a train in Chiapas that took us to the United States."

"But where on earth did you learn English?"

"There were missionaries in El Paraíso. One of them was from Georgia, which is why I thought this might not be such a bad place. But mainly I learned English from North American soldiers at the Salvadoran army base outside El Paraíso. Since I was eleven, I had been working there, mostly in the foreign advisers' billets, shining boots, cleaning the latrines. They were mostly good guys. They taught me a lot."

It was too much to absorb all at once. "Does Rea know all this?"

He shook his head. "Do not tell anyone what I'm telling you," he said.

"Why not?"

He didn't answer, but looked directly at me as though we were conspirators of some kind.

"What's it like there?" I asked. "In El Paraíso?"

"It's a regular place. Normal. Not like this, of course." He gestured past the booth we were in, past the chrome counters and plate glass windows, toward the traffic lights, the cars and trucks on the rain-washed streets.

"It's quiet, most of the time," he said. "Before the war, it was very quiet. Everybody worked hard in the fields. We had a plot of ground behind the *farmacia*. My family and two other families. Mother weeded the corn and beans. My father worked on the coffee *finca* of Don Jesus, odd jobs mostly, some carpentry work, taking care of the animals. I would help him or run errands. During harvest we all picked the coffee beans. We would also sort them and spread them out to dry in the sun. That was my favorite part, raking and turning the beans. When there was no work for us on the *finca,* we hung around the town square, waiting for trucks to unload. Or maybe the priest would hire us to prune the rosebushes or fix the garden gate. Or a crew from the telephone company would pay us a little to string wire or the power company to lay cable. We never had electricity until the month before I left, and then, because of the war, it was mostly off. They dug a well once, and my father and I helped put pipe in. The pump broke down, though, and last I heard they were still waiting for parts. I used to walk to the river and fill up plastic jugs for drinking water. My mother washed clothes in the river. She wove hats, too, so she could buy treats for the children and put a little in the offering plate for the poor."

It was not exactly what I had imagined.

"How many brothers and sisters do you have?"

"Living?"

That was an odd way to put it, I thought.

"Yes, living," I said.

"Three. My sister in Los Angeles. One brother with the guerrillas. The other with the army. They're both older than me."

"You had others who died?"

"Well, everybody in El Paraíso has children who die."

"Oh." But I didn't really know what he meant, and it was a line of questioning I didn't want to follow just then. "It seems like your parents would be awfully worried about you."

He glanced away. "My father died two years ago."

"In the war?"

He shrugged. "It's hard to tell what is the war and what is not. My mother is still alive. She is the housekeeper now for the priest. When enough time has passed, I can write her in care of him."

"Wow," I said.

"Wow?"

"I mean you've had such an interesting life."

He looked puzzled, like he suspected I might be making fun of him.

"I've never done anything or been anywhere," I said. This was not entirely true. I'd been to New York and Chicago and even spent a weekend in L.A. with my mother once, but that was nothing compared to picking coffee or riding in the back of a banana truck.

"But it's *your* life that's interesting to me," he said. "Your house is so grand."

"Grand?"

"The houses in my village are very small. And your father is an unusual man," Fernando said.

Unusual, I thought, is not the word. "What do you mean?"

"He's very gentle."

"Huh."

"I feel like I could tell him almost anything."

"I'm sure you could, Fernando. You're his patient."

"He is more than just a doctor of the heart, isn't he?"

"All cardiologists are trained in general medicine," I said, but I could tell that's not what he meant.

"It's almost as if he is a priest," Fernando said, glancing out across the sound at the staccato flashes of heat lightning that seemed to be approaching from the west.

I studied the scar that ran all the way from the point of his collarbone to the base of his skull. If you looked closely, you could even tell that it ran beneath the hair around his ear and ended just shy of his temple. I wondered what Fernando could want from Dad, and what Dad could want from Fernando, and what I really wanted from them both.

11

It started raining right as we crossed the causeway back onto the island, big, irregular drops, cold on my neck. Nothing had been decided in words, but I knew to keep straight past the turn to Rea's house; straight past the stables, where a light burned in the barn outside Trader's stall; straight past the house that looked like a bird, where maybe Dad was on the phone to one of his old lady patients; straight past the fork toward Christ's Church and Fort Frederica. We were headed to the darkness under the trees where the road ended at the point. We had outraced the rain, and the moon at the point was almost full where it had reappeared from behind a pair of flimsy clouds, each shaped like a parenthesis.

I cut the ignition and we stared straight ahead. I could smell, but not hear, the Atlantic. "Imagine," Fernando said, "that you are alone in the mountains and every leaf that moves is a spirit no bigger than your fist."

I closed my eyes and listened to the ticking of the cooling engine. "I think I'd be afraid," I said.

"Of course you would. So was I. But there's nothing wrong with fear. The more afraid you are, the more alive you are, or at least the world seems more alive."

"I've heard people say that, but I've never believed them. I don't like to be afraid. I don't even like horror movies."

He thought about that for a moment. "Neither do I."

"You have movies in El Salvador?"

"Of course. In the capital. The same movies you have here, only with subtitles."

I don't know why that surprised me, but it did. "I guess I must seem pretty naive to you," I said. He smiled and shook his head. "Look, Fernando, I don't want to pry, but I feel like something terrible happened to you in El Salvador."

He looked at his hands.

"I know how it is," I continued. "I mean, I don't know what you went through, but I know what it's like to have things you don't want to talk about. So you don't have to tell me anything. I just want you to know that if you ever want to talk to somebody, I'm a good listener."

We waited in the dark while a car stopped beside us, backed up, turned around, and left, its headlights sweeping the lowest branches of the trees.

"I don't mind telling you," he said quietly. "I want to tell you."

I looked at him, but I hadn't yet taken my hand off the wheel. A part of me wasn't sure I wanted to hear what he had to say, but another part of me had to know everything about him. His face was silhouetted against the moving clouds and the dark line of evergreen. His voice, when he finally began, was oddly serene.

"They attached the electricity here," he said, circling his thin wrist with his finger and thumb. "And the other wrist, too. They made me stand naked in a pan of salt water."

My head felt light. "Who did?"

"The Treasury Police."

"Where?"

"At their headquarters in the capital."

"But why? What had you done to them?"

"They were asking me the names of people in El Paraíso who sympathized with the guerrillas. When I said I didn't know any, they turned the electricity on."

The taste in my mouth was metallic. I tried to keep my voice level. "Did you finally tell them?"

"No. The people who sympathized with the guerrillas had left El Paraíso long before that. It was the truth, but the police didn't believe me."

"What else did they do, Fernando?"

"They took a medical instrument, like a dentist uses to pick at your teeth. They burst my eardrum with it."

There was this long silence. I could smell the rain coming. "It's just so horrible, so cruel." I didn't know what else to say, but I took his hand across the vinyl. It was fragile, yet sinewy, like the neck of a bird. A flare of heat lightning illuminated his face and the gray green leaves of the cabbage palms.

On an impulse, I touched his scar. I traced it from just shy of his temple all the way to his collarbone. It felt like something raw and alive. "Did they do that to you, too?"

He nodded. I felt the tears starting in the corners of my eyes, but I blinked them back.

"After the electricity?"

"After they saw they could not get any information out of me," he said. "I was useless to them after that, except as a message, so they blindfolded me and took me into the countryside with four others. They shot two of them in the head. They used the machete on the rest of us. I was found the next morning by a girl walking her pig to market. I was the only one still alive."

It was like somebody had kicked me in the stomach. I couldn't catch my breath. I closed my eyes and waited for the image to clear out of my head, but in my mind's eye I could still see the boys lying on the ground with their hands tied behind their backs, their bare heels touching, and Fernando crawling out from under the pile.

"The girl flagged down a sugarcane truck that took me to the hospital in the capital," he said. "I don't remember much about any of that. I just remember the rows of beds, the flies. When I got better, I sneaked out of the hospital and headed north. I didn't stop in El Paraíso. I just walked into the mountains and never went back."

"I can't believe what you've been through," I finally said.

He shrugged. "I am alive." And suddenly the rain howled down on us from behind.

I don't remember the ride back from the point until we got near the stables. We were both soaking wet, and I was freezing, but inside I was on fire with anger and humiliation. I didn't know where to direct any of it. It wasn't my pain, it was his, but somehow by telling me about it, he'd tangled up my life in it. War's one thing. Soldiers hunting other soldiers. Maybe I can understand that. But not torture. Not treating ordinary people worse than animals. I'll never understand that.

A tree was down at the Big Casino sign, and all the streetlights leading to the stables were out. That single light still burned in the barn by Trader's stall, though. When I pulled up in front of Rea's house, the rain had slacked. Fernando asked again if I wanted to come in. I shook my head, but I said I'd like to sit there for a minute. I had to get hold of myself. The wind still moved through the trees. Rea's yard was filled with small branches and debris, the lid from her neighbor's garbage can, two overturned lawn chairs.

"In the middle of it all," I finally said. "What were you thinking?"

"The electricity?"

"All of it. What was going through your head?"

"I was praying."

"For what?"

"That I would die."

"Of course," I said. "I would have, too."

"Yes, but there was something else," he said. He shifted in his seat, so he was facing me. "I don't know whether I can explain it to you, April. My English is not very good."

"Your English is perfect," I said. I wanted to tell him it was better than Rob Allard's. Better, in ways, than my own.

"I learned something while they were torturing me."

"What?"

"I learned that it is possible to remove yourself from yourself." He glanced to the side as if that wasn't quite right. "I learned that it is possible to step outside of your life."

"Outside of it?"

"Yes. You can become a stranger to it. And when you are a stranger to your own life, you see how sweet and sad it is. It's like a movie, and you are a character in it. At some point, you see that character praying that he will die. You feel for him, and you want to say, 'Don't worry. Everything is going to be all right.' From outside your life, you can know that."

"But from the inside you can't?"

"That's right. From the inside, it's all horrible, and all you can think about is getting out. But it is

95

possible to remove yourself. I think maybe you *have* to remove yourself in order to survive."

"I think I understand," I said.

"And there is something else, April. This is maybe the part you would call weird. These other people, the ones who are torturing you? From the outside of your life, you see that they are characters, too, who have their own roles to play out. They seem misguided and stupid, but you find yourself loving them in spite of what they're doing to you. You love them because they're part of your life, and you love your life. This is the important thing you find out when you step outside it. You find you love your life so much that you can make it through whatever happens, no matter how bad it gets. Because you see now there is a purpose to it."

"What?"

"Well, it is different for different people, I guess."

"For you, though, what was it?"

He scratched his eyebrow and took a deep breath. "To do what I am doing now."

"Sitting here with me?" I meant it as a joke, but it came out lame and flippant.

He was kind enough to take me seriously. "Well, yes. That and my work," he said.

"Your purpose in life is to work at the resort?"

"To make things grow," he said.

To make things grow. It took a second for that to settle in. And when it did, I felt like something had been lifted from my shoulders. It was so simple, I couldn't help but repeat it. " 'To make things grow?' You mean while you were being tortured, you were thinking about being a gardener?"

He nodded. "It is my gift," he said.

As I drove back down the road to Fort Frederica, my mind was on Fernando, on the terrible beauty of his life, so foreign and violent, but in ways so familiar to me. I thought about his hands, his birdlike wrists, his scar, his eyes. We hadn't kissed. We'd just said good-bye, and then he vaulted out of the Jeep. He didn't stop to turn until he was on the landing leading to his room. There he waved me on, his jeans so wet they clung to his thin legs. I thought then he was everything I had ever wanted, the cure for everything that was wrong with me. I waved back, but then waited until he disappeared and the light came on in his room. My hands were weak on the wheel as I pulled away from the curb.

I didn't know where all this would lead, but something had been sealed between Fernando and me. I knew that much at least, and I was turning it all over in my head, and so was unaware when some vague habit or intuition led me back to the stables. I parked the Jeep where I always did, under the live oak by the lunging pit. I could hear water running in the creek behind the barn. All the lights were off in the Commodores' trailer and their car wasn't there, although I thought the Jeep's headlights had reflected off something metallic under the trees at the back by the hot walker and the manure pile. I had it in my head that I would just go into the barn long enough to dry off in front of Mrs. Commodore's kerosene heater before I went home. It would be hard enough explaining to Dad where I'd been without dripping all over the floor.

I did not really notice that the door was unlocked, which it was, or that Rob Allard's denim jacket was hanging on a peg by the watercooler. The air inside, though, seemed close and overheated, and the single light outside Trader's stall appeared to bathe the aisle of the barn in an uncharacteristic, yellow light. Normally, I would have checked the horses first, but that night I didn't. I just went about the business of lighting the kerosene heater, but I was aware as I struck the match of the need to be quiet. I felt the same way I sometimes do in church, when an infant is being christened or communion is being served.

The blue and yellow flame sputtered soundlessly alive, and I turned to stand in front of the heater, my back to the radiating warmth. I could see Mrs. Commodore's calendar on the far wall, a collection of Tennessee Walkers, although that's not the breed she preferred. The legs of the horse in the January photograph, a high-headed roan, appeared to move in the flickering light from the heater.

I took a deep breath of the barn smell I loved, the hay and manure and animal sweat, but it didn't comfort me much. I was thinking about what Fernando's scar had looked like in the light from the Jeep's dashboard. His stories had rattled something out of me forever, some piece of trust I'd had that the world would be basically kind.

That's when I heard a sound from way down at the end of the barn, from one of the vacant pony stalls. It was not a startling noise, but soft and whispery. It could have been normal breathing, except for a certain raggedness there. And it carried with it a familiarity. I thought at first it was simply the sound of horses feeding. They sometimes nose and nudge the hay on the floor of their stalls, which would account for the softness and regularity. But the sound, after a little while, started to take a human shape.

Whatever it was, and by then I knew what it was, was old and reassuring, but at the same time shocking enough that I drew in my breath. It was someone, some couple, making love. Now I could hear her light, expectant gasps. A hard object repeatedly knocking against wood, a head, the heel of a boot, I couldn't tell, the sound of straw being rearranged in the same unwavering pattern. "I hear something," a female voice said as clearly as if it had originated in the same room I was in, and everything stopped.

"That was just Trader," he said. It was Rob.

"I don't care," she said. The sound started up again, like surf, like wind through leaves.

"I mean it," she said. I couldn't make out the rest. I twisted the valve on the heater to cut it off. I tiptoed to the door and eased out without disturbing a shadow. Outside, remnants of wind moved in the top branches of the live oaks. I had left the door of the

99

barn open and knew they would hear the Jeep crank, but some things cannot be helped. If it had been pavement I was leaving, the tires would have squealed.

12

When I got home from school the next afternoon, I saw a strange guy walking the property line between our house and the vacant lot next door, the side by the garage. He was short and balding, and he carried a clipboard in one hand. I thought he might be an insurance adjuster, checking on storm damage. Some limbs were down in the vacant lot, but it didn't look like any big deal to me.

"Miss?" he shouted as I wheeled my bike into the garage. I'd taken the bike for the exercise. I walked briskly out of the garage, pretending I hadn't heard the guy calling me, but he was standing in the driveway halfway to the back door.

"Are you by any chance related to Dr. John Hunter?" he asked. He was puffing a little. He had on a brown button-up sweater that ballooned at the waist and a tie with a New Orleans street scene on it.

"I'm his daughter," I said. "He's on a call, but he

101

should be driving up any minute." Actually, I didn't know where Dad was, but it was the answer I'd always given when I was home alone.

"Good. I need to talk to him." The guy blinked a couple of times. Then he glanced at his clipboard. "Now, you must be April."

"Are you a patient of his?"

"Oh no. I just need to ask him a few questions."

"Well, the door to his office is unlocked." I pointed to the stairs leading to the room above the garage.

"That's all right," the man said. "I'll just wait here on the stairs." He kind of waddled over to them and sat on the third step, adjusting his clipboard in his lap. He seemed harmless enough.

"Why don't you just come in for some coffee or a cold drink?"

"No," he said. "But thank you." And he smiled. His teeth were jagged and a little discolored.

I smiled back just enough to let him know I found him pleasant. Then I let myself into the kitchen. In the refrigerator I found some raspberry yogurt that hadn't gone bad. I hadn't been able to eat lunch at school because of the stories Fernando had told me the night before and what I'd heard in the stable afterward. I ate the yogurt with a big glass of ice water, standing at the sink, not to keep an eye on the guy in the brown sweater, but because that's where I always eat yogurt. It feels unnatural to me to eat anything out of a carton sitting down.

After I'd changed into my jeans and windbreaker

—I had to be at work at four—I checked the answering machine, one message for Dad, and looked out the window again. The man was gone, but Dad's station wagon was parked in the drive. I went outside. At first I didn't see them, but when I walked around back, I found them staring up at something in the live oak by the garage, a squirrel's nest, maybe? Then they walked toward the marsh, and I could see Dad gesturing with his hands, indicating a couple of things close in and then pointing off across the rivers and marshes toward Brunswick. I went back inside, brushed my hair into a ponytail and called the stables to let Mrs. Commodore know I might run late. I had to find out what Dad and the guy were talking about. Rob Allard answered the phone. He sounded bored as usual, so I knew he didn't suspect I'd been in the barn while he and his girlfriend were going at each other. Even now, the thought of it gave me the creeps.

"So are we talking about an hour, or what?" Rob asked.

"No. I'm talking minutes. There's something I've got to take care of at the house first."

"Right." He hung up without saying good-bye.

This time I walked straight up to Dad, with only a polite nod to the guy in the brown sweater, who was sweating around his temples, tiny beads like the condensation on a Coke can.

"There was a message for you from Mrs. Silkin." She was a patient of his with a thyroid disorder.

"I got it at the hospital, but thanks," he said. "Have you met Mr. Blake, April?"

"Not formally," I said, and shook the guy's hand. Like him, it was damp and a little puffy.

"I was telling Mr. Blake that we haven't seen our great blue heron for a few months now. Since November at least."

I nodded. A birder.

"April has to go to work," he said to Mr. Blake, "or she would tell you about the baby wrens."

"Yeah, I'm late already," I said.

"Where do you work?" Mr. Blake asked.

"Commodore Stables. It's just part-time. After school."

"What a wonderful job for a young woman."

"Yes. I like it a lot," I said.

"You probably meet interesting people there," he said, and he turned to Dad. "A surprising number of Hispanics are involved in horse breeding and training." Forget the bird business.

"Are they?" Dad said.

"We're just a riding stable," I clarified, a bit too quickly.

"Mr. Blake is from the Immigration and Naturalization Service, April," Dad said. "A very interesting line of work."

"I'm sure it is."

"You know about the I.N.S.?" Mr. Blake asked, and I must have blushed.

"Our history teacher said something about it," I lied. "We've been studying Ellis Island."

"Splendid."

Dad stuck his hands into his pockets and began rocking forward on the balls of his toes. "Don't let us keep you, sweetheart," he said. "Mr. Blake and I were just about to go in for coffee."

"I'll make it," I said. "I'm not really in a hurry to get to work. Besides, I'd like to ask Mr. Blake some questions. I'm thinking about doing a paper on immigration policy."

I excused myself and headed back into the house. I could feel Dad's eyes on my back. I don't know what kind of game he and I were playing. I suppose he was enjoying leading Mr. Blake on, pretending to be the affable small town doctor with nothing to hide. He probably wanted to find out exactly what Blake knew about Fernando. I wanted to find out what was going on, too, but I also wanted to make sure Dad didn't blow it. Just because you haven't had a drink in a year doesn't mean you've got all your wits back together yet.

Mrs. Commodore answered this time. I explained there was an emergency and Dad needed me to stick around a while longer. Mrs. Commodore didn't say anything right off the bat. She seemed to be turning something over in her mind. "Take all the time you need, April," she finally said in her tiny voice. "When you get here, I do want to talk to you, though. So just come to the office first."

"Yes, ma'am," I said. I was afraid she wanted to ask me about Rob and his girlfriend. The thought made my neck prickle. I felt like I was somehow implicated in all that.

I had just got the coffee on when Dad and Mr. Blake came in. "To tell the truth," Dad was saying, "I don't get many young males as patients. April can tell you that what we mostly see here are older women, widows mainly, with complaints that aren't limited to the heart."

"Some are," I said.

"Yes. Some are," Dad said. "What will you have with your coffee, Mr. Blake?" We were all three standing watching the carafe fill.

"Black, thank you," he said. "I particularly had in mind undocumented Central American refugees," he said.

"Hmm," Dad said. "And how would I know they were undocumented?"

Mr. Blake shrugged. "It's a small island."

"I'll be frank with you, Mr. Blake," Dad said. "I'm not sure whether I could reveal even a detail so trivial as country of birth about my patients. Medical records, you know, are confidential."

"I understand that," he said. "Although . . ."

"Here we are," Dad said. He insisted on pouring the cups. And when they had sat at the breakfast nook table, I continued to lean back into the counter, waiting for Dad to trap himself.

"You were saying?" he said to Mr. Blake.

"I was saying that I know medical records are confidential, but they can always be subpoenaed in court."

"I suppose they can," Dad said. I bet he was thinking about all his malpractice suits back in Atlanta. "Did you have a question, April?" he asked without turning. I figured he'd forgotten I was there, but no such luck.

"That's okay," I said. "I'm just soaking everything up."

Mr. Blake smiled a weak smile. Maybe something was starting to register with him, maybe not.

"But you *have* had patients from foreign countries," he said.

"Funny, but the first patients I saw on the island were Cuban," Dad said. "Mariel boat people." Mr. Blake nodded. "Coast Guard asked me to give them routine physicals. We had a Coast Guard headquarters here."

"I'm aware of that."

"Closed up the month after I came to the island."

"I'm sure they appreciated your cooperation," Blake said.

"They got my number from directory assistance."

"I suppose they didn't know you'd just gotten your license back."

"No, I don't suppose they did," Dad said. He took a sip of coffee. The steam curled above his head. "To tell the truth, I'm a little surprised *you* knew that. I don't think I mentioned it."

"It's a small island, Dr. Hunter," Blake said.

"Seems to be getting smaller by the minute," Dad said.

I glanced at the clock. It was four-thirty, but I wasn't about to leave now.

"So the Cubans haven't been the only aliens you've treated." The way he said the word "aliens" made it sound exactly like what it meant.

"I don't believe I said that," Dad answered. Careful, I wanted to tell him.

"I thought you had."

"No. Fact is, I don't feel comfortable about saying anything without checking my records carefully . . ."

"That won't be necessary," Blake said, "yet."

"April, you'd really better start heading to the stables . . ."

"I'm on my way." I didn't budge.

"There's nothing sinister in all this, Dr. Hunter," Blake said. He flipped to the second page of his clipboard. "We heard about an illegal who sought treatment in Jacksonville, doctor name of Cohen there, said a cardiologist on St. Simons had referred him. Otherwise vague about the details."

"Seems like you're going to an awful lot of trouble over one refugee."

"I know it seems that way," Blake said. He was stirring his coffee again and glancing out toward the marsh. The low sunlight fell in a diagonal line across his face. The sun had been intense after the storm. "We're working on a larger puzzle, a confidence scheme really, free-lancers collecting thousands of bucks from these refugees, claiming to be able to get them into the states with no problem and then ditching them at a railroad siding in hundred degree heat or sticking them on an overloaded, leaky shrimp boat that the Coast Guard's gonna catch anyway."

"How very humanitarian of you."

Mr. Blake seemed stung by this. He took a sip of coffee. "I'm just telling you the kind of case we're working on. I'm telling you more than I probably should. If you still want to think I'm some kind of bounty hunter tracking down undesirables so I can kick them out of the country, there's not much I can do to change that."

He was starting to sound too reasonable. "So what happens when you catch somebody?" I asked.

"We question them," he said. "We're interested in how they got here, what their circumstances are."

"And then?"

"If they're here illegally, they get a hearing. Everybody gets a hearing if they want one. Some of them wind up being here legitimately after all. Some of them can be granted political asylum, like these dissidents from the Soviet Union."

"And the rest?" Dad said.

"We deport some, sure. What do you expect me to say? There are laws, but the laws are changing all the time. I guess you read about the one Congress just passed."

Dad shook his head. He was starting to fade, his blood sugar falling. I looked at the clock above the sink. It was almost five, but I couldn't leave yet.

"Last week, Congress decided that Salvadorans in particular had gotten a raw deal in the hearing process. Seems to have been much easier to prove political repression in a place like Cuba, with a government we don't support, than in El Salvador."

"With a government we do support."

"Right. You understand the problem."

I didn't. I looked from Mr. Blake's face to the back of Dad's head.

"Congress rewrote the law," Blake said. "Made it easier, much easier, for Salvadorans to prove they'd be victims of persecution if we sent them home."

"It's about time," Dad said.

"Much easier," Blake repeated. "I'm only saying this . . ."

"In case I ever have any Salvadoran patients," Dad said. I thought I was going to come out of my skin.

"Right. Just in case. So that you might pass the word along."

Blake drained his cup. I could tell he was collecting himself to go.

"I'll check back with you every now and then," Blake said. "You speak Spanish right? You may hear something."

Dad got up, too. "How did you know that?"

Blake shrugged. "The island."

"Sure. The island," Dad said.

"What happens when they get back to wherever they're from?" I asked.

"Pardon me?" Blake said. He was buttoning his sweater.

"The ones you deport, the Salvadorans. What happens when they get home?"

"Oh. You're thinking about your paper now. Is it statistics you want?"

"I'm just curious," I said.

"You know something about Salvador?" he asked.

"No."

"Well, to be frank, April, I don't either. It's hard to keep all that stuff straight. Politics, you know. I can get you information, if you want it."

I started to shake my head, and then figured that would look weird, given everything else I'd said. "That would be fine," I said.

"You've got a nice little place here," Blake said to Dad.

"We take too much for granted, don't we?" Dad said.

"You've got that right."

They both paused at the door. They seemed to be waiting for something.

"Nice to meet you, April," Mr. Blake said. "Hope I can help you out with your project."

"Yeah, sure," I said.

"Crazy weather." He almost yodelled it.

"Give it a month," Dad answered. "You'll think crazy then."

I heard them on the stoop, still talking about nothing, just shooting the bull. Then I heard Mr. Blake's footsteps on the gravel. I saw him get into a beige Ford pickup at the end of the drive. Funny I hadn't seen it before.

When Dad finally came back in, I was pushing my way past him, jiggling my keys.

"What's wrong?" I heard him ask, but I didn't look back.

I just spat it over my shoulder: "I can't stand to watch you let yourself get jerked around like that."

13

Mrs. Commodore was leading Trader in from the turnout and I was following her, feeling contrite and a little nervous. She hadn't greeted me with her usual chirpy gossip. The barn seemed altered, like I'd been away for a while. I made a point of not looking down the aisle in the direction of the last pony stall, where Rod and his girlfriend had been going at each other the night before.

"Help me get him brushed and picked," Mrs. Commodore said.

"I'll just do it. It's my job."

"It's better if we do it together," she said. "We can talk."

She swung Trader around in the tack room so that he was centered under the brushes. She loosened the cavesson and the throatlatch while I unfastened the breast strap and the girth. Trader shivered all over when I slid the saddle off. He shifted his weight. His saddle pad was musty and damp with sweat.

"Leave the saddle on the table," Mrs. Commodore said. "I've got to file down those studs in the morning. I think they're rubbing."

I did what she said. "You aren't going to spray him?" I asked.

"Too cold. Besides, he doesn't need it. His rider didn't show."

"He's sweating some."

"Old horses will do that. Trader's not as old as Alfred, of course, but he's getting on up there. Next year may be his last in the ring." Mrs. Commodore chose a fine-bristle brush with a long handle. I tried to pick one as like it as I could. We both started at the head. Trader had a wild look in his eyes at first. I don't think he'd ever been brushed by two people at the same time, but the sound of Mrs. Commodore's voice calmed him. "Don't worry. You're still handsome," she said in her smallest voice. Trader's ears swiveled. I've noticed the horses never seem to have difficulty hearing her.

We took more time on his neck than we would have alone, waiting for whatever had to be said. When Mrs. Commodore finally spoke, it was not what I'd expected. "You know, I hardly think about love anymore," she said. "Mr. Commodore and I have been married thirty-six years. It was all tied up with horses. We didn't discover till later, maybe even after our oldest, Rick, was born—he's the lawyer in Dothan that we went to visit Christmas . . ." I knew all about Rick and the others. "It was after that, I think, that we really started to appreciate passion." Yes, so it would be about Rob and his girlfriend. I wondered how she'd found out.

"You probably think you know something about it already," she said.

"Not me." I picked a matt of ratted hair off the brush and started higher up the neck.

"Most young people think they do. But real passion comes later. When you start seeing what it is you're bound to lose. At least it did for Mr. Commodore and me."

I could hear the creak of the drying rack out back as it started and stopped. Rob must have been putting the beach ride horses on it one by one.

"When you're young, you think passion is the same thing as recklessness," Mrs. Commodore said. "Later, you find out it's just another way of giving comfort, maybe the best way, but still just a way. I'm six years younger than Mr. Commodore, and he turns sixty-one in March." I didn't know Mr. Commodore well. He had emphysema and was on oxygen twenty-four hours a day, but he had a portable tank that he rolled out to the stables sometimes.

"I guess I don't think about love now," she said, "because it's just the ocean we float around in. It's what holds us up. But I know how different it can be for people your age."

I jerked the brush through a tangle on Trader's belly. Normally I hate it when somebody talks about people my age. Like we had a disease, only we weren't smart enough to figure it out yet.

"You're standing on the edge," she continued, "getting ready to dive in. The water's dazzling, and so clear you think you can see the bottom. But you can't."

She stopped brushing. "I'd rather you not tell anybody exactly what I'm going to tell you now," she said. I wondered what words she would use. "The stables are kind of sacred to me."

"I know what you mean."

"I'm just a horsewoman," she said.

"I feel the same way." I was still brushing the soft, downy hairs of Trader's belly. Mrs. Commodore had taught me how to clean his sheath with a rag after pulling the foreskin back.

"Then maybe you'll understand," she said. "Somebody has told me about some goings-on at the barn at night." I felt a surge of self-righteousness.

"On Christmas Eve, two horses were ridden on the beach," she said.

I stopped brushing. Trader shook his head, maybe thinking we were through. I looked at Mrs. Commodore, the heat of shame rising in my neck.

"You know what I'm talking about, don't you, April?"

"Yes, ma'am." For the first time, my voice was smaller than hers. The heat hit my face. Sweat popped out in beads on my forehead.

"Then you also know that our insurance doesn't

cover pleasure rides after hours. The beach at night is a dangerous place for horses."

"I'm sorry," I said. "I knew I shouldn't have done it. It was like a Christmas present for a friend."

"I'm not interested in the circumstances," she said. "I'm sure you didn't mean any harm."

I smiled weakly, thinking she was going to forget about it, but she wasn't about to.

"I've thought about it and thought about it," she said. "I almost didn't say anything to you. I almost overlooked it. But like I told you, I'm just a horse-woman, April. It's the only thing I know. I can't let this pass, despite the way I feel about you."

I looked down at Trader's back, losing myself in a patch of rufous hairs tipped in white. It was like I had microscopic vision; I could see the smallest flakes of skin.

"You can either pick up this week's check or I can mail it to you. Maybe this summer I'll have more work for you, but I know I won't have any until then. I hope you understand. I just couldn't let this pass, no matter how much you wanted to please your friend."

She started brushing again, with renewed vigor. I looked at my brush. I thought about laying it on the table and walking out without another word. The barn was absolutely quiet except for the distant creak of the drying rack. A murderous impulse seized me when I thought about Rob Allard calmly watching the horses turn the rack in the cool evening air. But I squelched it. I could never tell Mrs. Commodore what I knew about him, even after what he'd just done to me. He was too despicable for words. I shook my head. Then I picked up the rhythm of Mrs. Commodore's brushing. Afterward I plaited Trader's tail, while she picked the hooves, and I taped his tail up in a sock so it wouldn't get all messed up during the night.

"Good night, April," she said when we were finished. "Maybe I'll see you come summer. Nobody needs to know any more about this than you want to tell them yourself."

"I appreciate that," I said.

"I will miss having you to talk to," she added, and then she was gone, waddling down the aisle past the stalls where the horses hung their heads out expectantly for her.

The windows in the upstairs of Rea Britt's house were dark, but I went to her front door anyway. The night had turned cold, and the star Sirius was so bright it wavered like a far-off fire. Rea was home. I could tell that from the blue flicker of her TV against the living room wall. She turned the porch light on, and I could see the outline of her hips through her flannel nightshirt when she opened the door. She was holding a Kleenex to her nose, and her hair was uncombed. She acted like she had been expecting me.

I followed her into the living room, which was barely furnished with a few pieces of rattan and a couple of elongated African sculptures. Her cat, Elvis Two, lay on his back in the center of the floor, pawing at the fringe of a rug Rea had told me she'd picked up in Peru.

Rea's back was to me, her hip cocked. She stared at the television as though she suspected it might move. It was the public broadcasting channel, and a man in a black wool cap was reciting a poem we'd studied in Mr. Noonan's lit class about a center that wouldn't hold.

"Is Jack all right?" Rea finally asked.

"I don't know. I mean, I'm sure he is," I said. "I just came from the stables."

She turned. "So you haven't talked to him?"

"Not since five or so. Why?"

"Fernando's gone."

"What do you mean Fernando's gone?"

"I thought you already knew. I thought that's why you came. Sit down," she said. "I have some tea steeping in the kitchen."

"Where'd he go?"

"I don't know. I'll tell you everything I know when I come back."

She disappeared into the kitchen, and I stared at Elvis Two. Fernando was gone, I thought to myself, but it hadn't really sunk in yet.

When Rea came back, she was carrying a tray with a teapot shaped like a peacock and two tiny blue cups. "Sugar?"

I shook my head.

"After Mr. Blake from the I.N.S. visited you this afternoon, he came here," she said. "He struck me as a nitwit. Thankfully, his questions were vague enough. I told him as little as possible. I didn't realize Fernando was upstairs in his room. He must have been listening. When Blake left, I called your father, to compare notes." She finished pouring the tea and handed me mine. "Later, I thought I heard Fernando on the outside stairs, so I went up to let him know what had been going on."

I took a sip of the tea, black currant. It was scalding.

"Fernando's room was empty, I mean stripped of everything that belonged to him. He didn't have much to begin with, but his clothes were gone, and his clock radio, and his books. He'd made the bed, as he always does, and there were two notes in envelopes on the pillow, one for me and one for you."

The teacup shook in my hand. I set it with a rattle onto its saucer. Elvis Two glanced at me with studied alarm and then turned back to the TV, where the man in the wool cap was howling his way through another poem.

Rea retrieved the envelope from the mantel and handed it to me. I didn't open it then, and I could tell from her expression that she didn't expect me to.

I had come to confide in her about losing my job, and to see if Fernando was at home, but now the job seemed meaningless, less than meaningless. "Thanks for the tea," I said. "I'd really better go."

"I understand," she said. "I didn't realize you and Fernando were such good friends." There wasn't a trace of accusation in her voice. She was his friend, too, after all.

My throat felt like it was closing, and I resisted the impulse to hug her. She walked me to the door. Behind her the blue light of the TV flickered crazily on the walls. Elvis Two turned when Rea opened the door. His eyes flashed yellow and then went out.

I walked to the Jeep under moonlight and drove home through streets that were totally deserted. I ripped the envelope open in the kitchen after I'd made sure Dad wasn't there. It was a blue piece of lined notebook paper, torn from a binder. Except for the "Dear April," the message was in Spanish.

In a fit of frustration, I thought about calling Dad at the hospital, where I was sure he must have gone, but then I remembered seeing a Spanish-English dictionary in the bookcase by his bed, where he kept all his Central American junk. It took me a while to put it together, and I probably wouldn't have been able to if I hadn't remembered something from that one semester of Spanish I took at my old high school in Atlanta.

"*Búscame en la luz,*" the note read. "Look for me in the light."

14

I knew Fernando had to mean the lighthouse, but I checked the phone book just in case, to make sure there wasn't some store or restaurant with *light* in the name that I hadn't thought about. There wasn't, so I headed out again in the Jeep toward the village. It had turned a serious cold now. I could see my breath, and I still hadn't figured out how to get the top up, so I wore a double layer of sweaters and a toboggan cap, a black and yellow one that Dad had worn in college. It's like him to hang on to something that long, when he can't keep track of his car keys or his glasses. He lost his birth certificate, his army discharge papers, and the deed to our house in Atlanta all at the same time. But he's kept track of his Georgia Tech cap and sweatshirt and a meerschaum pipe he smoked in the army. That's about all from his past, except me and photos, that he has left.

The restaurants and yogurt shop at the village

were still open. The clothing and hardware stores had closed at six, and the playground had that sad winter look to it, swings swaying in the cold wind off the water.

I walked past the deserted benches and playground equipment toward the lighthouse. Its beam had just swung around. The gate around the old lightkeeper's cottage was unlocked, but the door to the lighthouse, the one the tourists use, wasn't. The sign said the hours were eight in the morning until five in the afternoon. I went around back. The maintenance door was barred and bolted. I tried to peer inside the ground-floor window, but the glass was glazed. Fernando wasn't there, anyway. I could feel his absence. It's always been like this for me; I'm my father's daughter, I find something one day and lose it the next.

I went out on the public pier—it's a little frightening even in daylight—and I leaned against the railing and into the wind. The moon was out, nearly full but high and remote. I spat into the waves that were washing against the pilings. If you watch that action long enough, you can get lost in it.

I heard the creak of steps behind me, a couple of gay guys. I'd seen them kissing in a parked car behind the Jitney, Jr., on the road to Fort Frederica. Love will make you seek out places like that. I said hello when I passed them. They smiled, but I could tell I was nothing to them, a girl's voice on the pier.

I was broke, but I had a kind of friend named Deidre Holloway who worked at the yogurt shop and gave me credit. She kept a running count on the back of a Sea Island tourist map. I say a kind of friend, because the yogurt shop was the only place we knew each other. I saw her at school sometimes, but we didn't have any of the same classes, and when we saw each other in the halls, we just didn't say much. Deidre had a pale, moon-shaped face with freckles, and hair so fine you wondered how she kept it in place.

"We're out of raspberry," she said when I walked in.

I was surprised she had recognized me in Dad's cap, which I took off. "What about French vanilla?"

"That's easy enough." She already knew I wanted it in a small cup, with sprinkles. It's the kind of place where you get your water yourself out of the fountain under the bulletin board. I always check the board, there's never anything there, a lot of business cards for people who saw limbs off trees and your friendly insurance agents, who always add a little note with an exclamation point after it.

"I don't know how you can eat something cold on a night like this," Deidre said.

"Nothing else to do," I said.

"You're eighteen, aren't you?"

"No."

"Well, Petie at the 7-Eleven sells underage, don't tell anybody I told you that."

"I don't drink."

"Oh, I know. I don't like the way the stuff tastes, either." She didn't get it. She slid the yogurt to me. I started eating it standing up. "I just do it when everybody else does," Deidre added. "Beer, mainly. Every boy that takes me out has this thing about beer."

I nodded in agreement. My tuba player in Atlanta, for one.

"How's business been?" I asked.

Deidre shrugged. "You're the only person who's come in on my shift."

"Maybe it's the cold."

"Yeah," she said. "That or the flu. It's going around, you know."

I looked up at her. I had a mouthful of sprinkles or I would have said something.

"I think I'm coming down with it," she said. She shook the glasses by their stems, they were for sundaes that nobody but the yuppies ordered, and set them on a red and white towel to dry. Her hands were creamy and white, like lady fingers. I wondered how many times she'd been told that she could have men eating out of her hand. With me, it had always been: "You have such a wonderful smile. I just wish we could see it more often."

"Either I'm coming down with the flu," she said, "or I just didn't get enough sleep last night." She glanced at the window. I turned, thinking somebody was fixing to come in, but it was just our reflections in the glass. Hers looked a little shy and dumbstruck, like a cow in a car's headlights.

When I turned back around she said, "I had a date last night. I shouldn't have stayed out so late."

"Depends on the date," I said.

She reddened and looked at her hands.

"I've got to ask you something real important before I forget it," I said. "I'm looking for a guy . . ."

"Aren't we all," she said.

"You'd know him if you saw him. He's a foreigner, thin, dark."

"Got a scar on the side of his neck?" Deidre said.

"Right. His name's Fernando. Have you seen him tonight?"

"No. He doesn't come in here, but he passes by every night, on his way to the pier, I guess. He kind of nods, and I wave back." This made me unreasonably jealous. "He's cute in an odd way, but he can't be a day over fifteen. How do you know him?"

"He's a patient of my father's. Don't tell anybody I said that, though. I think it's confidential."

She shrugged. "Who's to tell?"

"If you see him, tell him I need to talk to him. Tell him I'm not sure what he meant."

"What he meant?"

"He'll understand. Tell him to call me. There's nothing to worry about."

"I'm not worried," Deidre said.

"There's nothing for *him* to worry about. Tell him that."

"Your yogurt's melting."

I had turned so that I could see the street in case Fernando walked by, but I was trying to be unobtrusive. Deidre came out from behind the counter and walked over to the jukebox. She took two quarters from her smock and selected a couple of songs. The

126

first was a sentimental country western addressed to a girl the singer's never seen.

Deidre had turned to face me. She was leaning back into the jukebox, the amber lights catching her face from underneath. "You work at the Commodore Stables, don't you?" she asked.

"That's right," I said. I didn't have it in me to tell her I'd been fired that very afternoon.

"Tell me everything you know about Rob Allard," she said.

It took a second for me to make the connection, and when I did, I felt that wave of queasiness again. It had been Deidre's voice in the barn. I looked back down at my yogurt. Oh, Deidre, I thought, you poor sucker. But all I said was, "There's not much to tell."

A yuppie couple with three kids came into the yogurt shop at just that moment. They were a good excuse to get out of there fast, before Deidre figured out what I knew about her and Rob.

15

The air outside was cold and clear. A lighted barge moved silently across the sound. I pulled on my toboggan cap, jammed my fists into my windbreaker and headed for the beach. It was low tide. The surf was so distant, it seemed inconsequential. After the closeness of the shop, though, the beach and the night took my breath. The faster and farther I walked, the lonelier it got, until the village was nothing but a string of lights behind me, the beach houses all vacant until spring.

I was coming up on the rock jetties, where the beach took a turn and curved north toward the deserted Coast Guard station. It was the spot where Fernando and I had stopped our horses, and the beam from the lighthouse had raced up the beach toward us. I turned and saw that the beam had swung out toward Jekyll now. It was visible in the salt spray above the sound, which held the light like particles of ice before it dropped them into the surf.

When I turned back around, I saw the silhouette of a boy sitting on a rock higher up toward the dunes. He immediately got up and, crouching, scrabbled away crablike over the rocks. He had startled me, but there was something familiar about the way his jacket rode up in back.

"Fernando!" I shouted.

He stopped and stood erect. I pulled off my toboggan cap and motioned him to come down. He was hugging himself against the cold when he got to me.

"I didn't recognize you with your cap on," he said. "I didn't think you were going to come."

"How was I supposed to know what you meant? I thought you were talking about the lighthouse."

"I was." At that instant, the beam illuminated us again. Fernando's face sprang from the dark like something brought suddenly to the surface of water. It was even more fragile than I had remembered, the scar more vivid, and his expression was filled again with something like remorse.

"I've been worried about you," he said.

"Worried about *me?* What about *you?*"

"I'm fine. I've found a place to hide." The light had moved on.

"Where?"

He pointed in the direction we were already headed, past the jetties toward the abandoned Coast Guard station.

"How'd you get in?" I asked.

"There is a door to the cellar. It was locked, but I took the hinges off. It's not the first time I've had to hide. In the mountains, we slept in tunnels."

"But what are you going to eat?"

He shrugged. "I don't need much."

"And your job?"

"I cannot ever go back there."

Fernando walked with his head bent forward, as though into a wind.

"Rea was surprised that you'd gone," I said. I wanted to add that I was, too.

"I left a note for her, like the one for you, to let her know where she could find me. I heard everything he said to her, the man from the immigration service."

"He came to our house, too."

"What did you tell him?"

"Nothing."

"He told Miss Britt he wanted to question me. In Salvador when they question you, they blindfold you first."

"It's not like that here." I'm not sure I believed that myself.

"Sometimes in El Salvador they give you a shot of something to make you talk, or they just tighten a wire around your neck."

I took his elbow. "This isn't El Salvador."

He gently slipped out of my grip. "It is a kind of El Salvador, isn't it?" He was walking ahead of me now.

"Look, I don't know what it's like to be who you are," I said. "I just want to be able to see you."

He stopped and turned, waiting for me to catch up. "I want to see you, too," he said. "But we have to be careful, April. It is more complicated than it was before. More dangerous. You have to watch everything you say. And sometimes, even if you don't say anything, they can read the truth in your eyes. You have to learn to control your eyes."

We were approaching the Coast Guard station now, much larger and more desolate in the dark. A cockeyed shutter flapped in the breeze off the sound.

"I don't think I could ever learn to control my eyes," I said.

"You can do anything when your life depends on it. You can learn to control your breathing and the sounds your stomach makes. You can become a rock if that will help keep you alive."

We climbed silently up the dune toward the Coast Guard station. I followed him to the side, where the two halves of the cellar door looked tightly secured by a heavy rusted lock. Fernando took something from his pocket, a screwdriver or pocketknife, and stooped to loosen one of the hinges. The metal fell free with a clatter. He opened the door onto darkness and looked up at me.

"Once we are all the way in, I can turn on the flashlight. You will have to feel your way until then."

He stood, and the beam of the lighthouse swung around again. It didn't reach us up on the dune, but fell in a thin path onto the beach below.

Then Fernando led me down the steps. I felt for the end of each one with my toes. At the bottom of the steps, we stopped to let our eyes adjust. Gradually, the room began to take shape. Moonlight seeped through cracks in the plank flooring above and fell in dim, oblong blocks through the holes where the heating and cooling vents had been.

Fernando turned on his flashlight, which had red plastic taped over the front. In its reddish glow, I could clearly see the dimensions of the cellar. It was only half finished and exhaled an odor of old dirt. To my right was a couch with a floral slipcover facing a dart board hung crookedly on the wall. In the corner stood a rusted drink machine, the kind that lay flat and could have been filled with ice. The floor was lighter in a large rectangle in the center of the room —where a pool table had been, or one for Ping-Pong. The cellar must have been a kind of break room. I imagined the Coast Guardsmen clattering down the stairs after lunch for a quick game of eight-ball and icy Cokes. It was an ironic home for an illegal alien. But somehow appropriate, I thought.

"Where's all your stuff?" I asked him.

"Stuff?"

"Your clothes and things."

"I got rid of most of it, put it in a garbage can outside the library. It was too much to carry. But my radio's over there. I can get a station from Miami in Spanish, and of course Radio Havana, although really I don't much like to listen to that. It's all for show."

"Do you have a bathroom in here?"

"The water is off, but you know the bathhouse down by the beach?"

I nodded.

"I use it in the morning before sunrise and after dark. Other times, there are always the dunes, but I have to be careful not to be seen."

"Where do you sleep?"

"The couch."

If I hadn't known, I would never have guessed that someone was living in the cellar. Except for his radio and a change of clothes folded neatly on the couch beside a few books, the place was as empty as a tomb.

"We can go upstairs now," he said. "The moon is high enough that we will not need this." He flicked off the flashlight, and I followed him up the staircase onto the main floor. The moon had risen above the ocean, and it filled all the windows with light. Moonlight touched a recruitment poster the guardsmen had left behind and fell in sheets on their abandoned desks. Tacked to a bulletin board was a navigation chart, which looked vaguely celestial in the silver light. I was aware, too, of the smell. This was a place men had vacated not that long before, but don't ask me to describe the smell. It was not unpleasant is all I mean.

"Have you ever been to the top?" he asked.

I shook my head. He meant the control room, where the Guardsmen scanned the horizon with binoculars. It was what gave the station its magnetism for the boys on the island my age, who must have envisioned themselves sitting up there in their fresh uniforms, staring out to sea.

Fernando insisted I go first this time—it was just a few steps. The control room had been stripped of electronic equipment and furniture. All that remained was a swivel-backed typing chair and an upended wooden Coke box that Fernando must have brought up from the cellar. The view was spectacular from all sides—the undulating grass of Bloody Marsh glimmering before the dark trees and house lights of the island's interior, the village with its lighthouse about to swing around, and the ocean, of course. The moonlight on the water was like fish scales, and far off an oil tanker winked red and green, while close in, above the trees, the bats dove.

We stood there for a long time, just admiring the view, and then I sat on the floor with my back to a windowsill. Fernando sat down beside me. We weren't touching, but I could feel him, as though he were radiating heat.

"Would you like something to eat?" He held up a can of Vienna sausage.

"No. I had a late lunch at school," I said. "And Dad's expecting me back."

"Did your father name you April?"

"It was my mother's idea," I said. "My father wanted something plainer, like Ann or Beth."

"In El Salvador, your name might be Maria de las Flores, Maria of the Flowers."

"I like that."

"It's all right, but much too common for you,"

he said. "April is better. April Hunter. It sounds like a constellation."

I looked over at him, into the face I'd memorized by heart. "I can't believe I ran into you."

"Ran into me?"

"It's a figure of speech. Nothing was going right for me until I met you."

"How can you say that? You have everything."

"I know it must look that way to you," I said. "But I don't have everything, Fernando. Something's out of whack with my life."

"Out of whack?"

"Another figure of speech. It means something's wrong. I don't know what. The island just hasn't worked out for me."

"Why did you come here in the first place?" he asked.

"My dad quit drinking a year ago."

"But why did you come here?" he repeated.

"To help him."

"To help him what?"

"To help him get back to normal."

"Normal," he repeated. He looked toward the windows and smiled. "In Spanish, we pronounce it nor*mal.* If you hear a weapon firing in the middle of the night, and someone asks, 'What was that?' you say, 'Nothing. It's nor*mal.*' Or if a child finds a body in the ravine outside your town, you don't act surprised. 'It's nor*mal,*' you say, and your neighbors reply, *'Sí, es normal.*' "

"I guess you can get used to anything," I said.

He looked back at me. "No, April, there are some things you never get used to. You act like you're used to them because you want to survive, but when you use a word like 'nor*mal,*' you're saying just the opposite of what you seem to be."

"Do you think I could learn Spanish?" I asked.

"Of course," he said. "Spanish is easy. The secret is to speak directly from the heart."

"Isn't that what we've been doing?"

I think this must have embarrassed him at first. He looked again toward the windows, the moonlight reflecting in his eyes, and I felt that sharp pain I associate with desire. I think it is the pain of knowing that what you desire can never be yours completely. Not even in the moment you possess it do you possess all of it. And it's impossible to hold on to even that for very long. You glimpse what you desire coming toward you, you glimpse it moving away from you. Or you watch it scatter into the air like bits of debris, until what you desire is all around you and impossible to hold. I know all this now. I didn't know it then. At that moment, I thought I could have exactly what I wanted simply by wanting it bad enough.

When Fernando turned back, he put his fingers under my chin and kissed me lightly. I could tell he was nervous. His chin trembled.

He kissed me again, and we looked at each other. "Put your head in my lap," I said. I took off my windbreaker and rolled it up and put it in my lap. Then I scrunched up a little so he'd be comfortable.

He stretched out on the floor with his head on the windbreaker, and it felt right to me.

My hair had come loose and was hanging over Fernando like a kind of canopy. His eyes looked up into mine, they were deep and clear, and I cradled his head closer against my stomach. I couldn't seem to get him close enough.

"Do you have to work after school tomorrow?" he asked.

"I'm not working anymore, for a while anyway. Mrs. Commodore found out we took the horses for a ride on Christmas Eve."

"I'm sorry," he said.

"It's not your fault. I'd do it again. I wouldn't take anything for that night."

"That must be another figure of speech."

"It means the moment was valuable to me. Important. It was more than just a good time."

"It was the same for me," he said.

"We say things like that only happen 'once in a blue moon.' "

"What does that mean?"

I thought about it a minute and realized I didn't know. I leaned over and kissed him again. His lips tasted of cinnamon and salt. I felt his hand behind my head. His touch was delicate, but strong, and suddenly I couldn't get enough of his mouth, which was soft and seemed to fit mine perfectly, and he seemed to know just where I needed to go and what I wanted to do when I got there.

16

(The next day Mr. Noonan wanted to talk about *Hamlet,* but nobody seemed interested in Ophelia's madness. Except for me and Rob Allard, who had seen the video, nobody even knew who Ophelia was. It's amazing, though, once they get going, how earnestly a class can enter a discussion about something they've never read. And why the teachers don't catch on is beyond me. Or maybe they know and just play dumb. Anyway, Mr. Noonan was as energetic as a cheerleader as he diagrammed Hamlet's predicament and the course of Ophelia's madness on the board. The questions he asked had the answers imbedded in them, so of course he found interesting observations from all over the room.

I was just thankful to be sitting in the back corner of the room, where I could daydream. The high school's an old one, Glynn Academy in Brunswick. The advanced lit room has enormous windows on both sides that, if you're in the corner like I am, bathe your desk with light.

The other good thing about sitting at the back was that Rob Allard was sitting at the front. Mr. Noonan had moved him there at the beginning of the year, for what he said was a wandering eye. The truth is, Rob Allard was flunking advanced lit, and how he got into the class in the first place I'll never know. He had never turned in a paper he'd written himself or an exam he hadn't copied from someone else. The rest of the class knew it, too, but I guess they felt sorry for him. I didn't feel sorry one bit.

"What do you think, April?" Mr. Noonan asked.

"I'm sorry. I didn't catch the question."

"Rob thinks Ophelia has what he calls 'this thing for her father.' "

"Polonius?" I asked, incredulous.

"That *is* her father's name, April."

"I know, but where does he get that from?"

"Why don't you tell her, Rob?"

The fact is, I knew where he'd gotten it, from confusing Polonius with Oedipus, and then switching genders. He'd never read *that* play either.

"Everybody's heard of the Polonius complex," Rob said in all seriousness, but when the class laughed, he acted like he'd intended it as a joke.

"Well, her father doesn't have anything to do with her madness," I said, "and besides, I don't think she's really mad."

"You don't?" Mr. Noonan's eyebrow quivered.

"I mean, not in a clinical sense." Someone in the class went "oooh."

"It could just be P.M.S.," Lyle Kendall piped in.

"Haven't you ever wanted to kill yourself?" I asked Lyle, intending it for the whole class.

"No," he said. "Have you?"

"It was a rhetorical question," I said.

"Well, mine wasn't, and you didn't answer it," Lyle said.

"We're talking about a play," I said, "and a young woman who's beside herself with the grief of being alive."

Another oooh.

"Are you saying Ophelia could have avoided her fate?" Mr. Noonan asked, surprisingly subdued now that he knew someone clearly had read the play.

"Yes. I'm saying if she had been able to find the kernel of joy in the grief of being alive, yes, I'm saying she might not have killed herself."

"The joy in the grief of being alive?" Mr. Noonan repeated, and I felt like an absolute fool.

"I don't know what I mean," I said.

"Tell *me*," Lyle said.

"No, that's fine, April, an interesting observation," Mr. Noonan said. "Maybe it goes beyond the bounds of the play, though, because Ophelia *does* kill herself after all, some say for love, some say in spite of love. We'll talk more about that and other elements of the play tomorrow. But these are all interesting points you've raised." Mr. Noonan turned to erase the board, and his shoulders slumped.

★ ★ ★

As fate would have it, I ran into Deidre on the sidewalk on the way to lunch. Glynn Academy is more like a college campus than a typical high school. The old buildings, at one time separate schools, are grouped together around grassy squares. The street's been blocked off from traffic. Beyond it is the spire of a church steeple, the docks along the river, and the smokestacks of the paper mill. My high school in Atlanta was brand spanking new, an architecture they call post-modern, but which to me looked like the outside of a discount shoe store. The walls were mauve and the rooms so acoustically perfect you could hear your heart crashing in the middle of an exam. But Glynn Academy's walls were painted yellow, the ceilings at least fourteen feet high; the floors were red tile instead of carpet, the kind of tile that makes your heels click and echo when you're late to class.

That's what I was thinking about, Ophelia and the sound of heels on red tile, when I saw Deidre with her foot propped up on one of the cement benches under the school's biggest live oak. Her strawberry blond hair hung like a veil, almost obscuring her face. She was tying her laces. She had on Keds and a pleated blue skirt, nothing like what the other girls wore. Deidre and I didn't know each other at school. But today, I stopped and waited for her to look up. When she did, she gave me a kind of broken up smile, like it was something she'd been saving too long, and so didn't come out just right.

141

"Still no raspberry, huh?" I asked.

She shook her head.

"They ought to put yogurt machines in the cafeteria," I said.

"Well, I can't eat the stuff anymore. Working at the shop killed my appetite for it. Did you ever find your friend?"

At first I didn't know what she meant, and then I remembered Fernando with that sweet jolt you get when you've found something you thought you'd lost. I was going to see him again that afternoon, but I couldn't tell her that, so I just nodded.

"Are you on your way to lunch?" I asked.

"Yeah."

"So am I. Why don't we eat together?"

Deidre glanced toward the main building, so I added, "Unless you're going to sit with Rob."

"No. He's got shop this period." She smoothed her skirt. I could tell she was uncomfortable, having bought a size too small.

"How long have you been, uh, seeing Rob?" I asked. We were headed across the street toward the cafeteria.

"Four months."

"Huh, I didn't realize that."

"It's been real intense. I know that Rob dates a lot of girls, or used to."

I had a mental flash—the rich girls from Sea Island, the twelve year olds at the stables, him wanting to give me a ride in his classic Corvette. "All men are dogs," I said.

"Women, too, don't you think?"

I shrugged. How could I talk sensibly with a girl unlucky enough or with bad enough taste to be hooked on Rob Allard?

We swung the cafeteria doors open, and I knew in a flash it was fish sticks and macaroni and cheese.

"Gag a maggot," Deidre said, and I remembered she was from California and was new to the island like me, and that her stepfather worked at FLETC, the Federal Law Enforcement Training Center, in Brunswick.

Fortunately, because we were running late, there were plenty of tables by a window overlooking the outdoor basketball courts. A couple of the guys from advanced lit were in a ragged pick-up game beneath the shadow of the school's old steam plant. We gave them the once over and then concentrated on getting our food down before the bell.

"The boy with the scar," she said. "I'm sorry. That sounds crude."

"No, that's fine."

"Are you seeing him, or just friends?"

"I just met him," I said, but I could tell that didn't satisfy her curiosity.

"I guess it's hard to tell at first," she said. "How it's going to pan out."

"That's right."

"I knew about Rob from the start, though."

Oh spare me this, I thought.

"His car was broken down . . ." Not the classic Corvette! I thought. ". . . so we walked to the video store and rented *Lawrence of Arabia*. It was four hours long." She looked dreamy-eyed, as though a war movie with ten thousand camels in it was cause for celebration.

"Then what?" I asked innocently.

"Then he walked me back home. We held hands. I fell like a ton of bricks."

At just that moment, Mr. Noonan walked up. He'd brought his lunch, as always, in a brown paper bag, and he'd just gotten a styrofoam cup of iced tea to take back to his room.

"Excuse me, ladies," he said. Give me a break. "I just want you to know, April, that I've been thinking since class . . . your comment about Ophelia." He said this with enormous sadness in his voice, like I'd told him to get lost. His eyes were vague and unfocused, and his mustache was quivering again. "I wonder how you came by that insight."

It sounded like he thought I had plagiarized something, but I quickly chalked that up to my own paranoia. "It just hit me," I said. "I really don't know what I meant."

"Perhaps that's the paradox of insight. We never appreciate it at the moment. It's only later, as events reveal themselves, that we understand how clearly we saw the problem right off the bat."

"I suppose so," I said.

"You might want to develop your idea into a topic for your term paper," he said, but I knew that wasn't what he was driving at.

"Thanks. I'll think about that."

"Good. Well, I have a peanut butter and banana sandwich waiting for me."

"Well, 'bye," I said, and he smiled and walked off.

The pick-up basketball game had dispersed, the bell was about to ring. The cafeteria, in fact, was suddenly empty except for me and Deidre. I realized that as irregular and tentative as our friendship had been, when you got down to it, she was probably the only girl on the island I could really call a friend.

"I was about to tell you some news. I should have told you last night. Rob asked me to marry him," she said.

I set my fork down, real slow. "He what?" I whispered.

"He's going to join the Coast Guard after graduation. As soon as his training period's over and he gets stationed permanently, we're hoping it's Savannah, of course, but wherever it is, when he gets stationed there, we're going to get married."

"Rob told you this?" I asked.

"Sure. Don't you think that's great?"

The bell rang. A dozen or more swallows swooped down from the stack above the old steam plant and did a mad little mid-air ballet above the basketball courts.

"Sure, I do," I said.

17

After school, I stopped by the stables to pick up my check. It was not the easiest thing I have ever done. Missy Trainor, who usually works only on Sunday afternoon, was saddling up Trader to take my place in the ring. She had cinched his bit strap too tight, and while she wasn't looking, I loosened it. Then I stroked Trader's forehead and held my face up to his. It's not my imagination that he smells different from the other horses, a sad but clean smell that reminds me of attics. There was no way to let him know that this was my last day at the stables. I just patted him on the neck so hard the dust flew and then left the tack room before Missy got back with a clean saddle pad.

The office door was ajar. Mrs. Commodore usually keeps the checks in a wire basket on the desk, where anybody can walk in and steal them. She has a theory that things left in full view are always the safest. I flipped through the half dozen checks in the basket, but didn't see mine. Just then I heard the sound of rubber wheels on wooden planks, Mr. Commodore pulling his portable oxygen tank into the barn. I didn't know him well at all and so was frightened and a little put off by the paraphernalia associated with his illness. He had plastic tubes up his nose, for instance, and a bandage on his forearm from a botched attempt to start an IV line. I wasn't even sure he would recognize me, but he waved as he passed the door, his arm as skinny as a chicken leg. I waved back.

I finally thought to look in Mrs. Commodore's stack of outgoing mail, and that's where I found my check. It was for a little more than I had figured. When I turned to go, I almost ran smack into Rob Allard, who was carrying a handful of new insurance forms. I couldn't tell which of us was more embarrassed, but I was determined to be the first to speak and so keep control of the conversation.

"Congratulations," I said, without any of the irony I felt.

"What for?"

"You and Deidre. She told me you were engaged."

"I didn't know you knew her," he said.

"I don't, very well, but she seems very nice."

"She is," he said. He slapped the stack of insurance forms on the desk and thumbed through them, as though to get a count. It galled me to no end that he could just stand there without one word of apology for costing me my job.

"How far along *is* she?" I asked.

Rob looked up, stung. "That's a shitty thing to say."

I shrugged.

He turned back to the forms. "Deidre's not pregnant," he said, "and it wouldn't be any of your business if she were."

I smiled. "Just asking," I said, and I was out of the office, out of the barn, into the clean light and the air that was too cold even for January.

"Hey, you wait a minute," I heard Rob call after me. "Who told you she was pregnant?" But it was too late. I was already drunk on the sweet taste of revenge.

Still flying high on the panic in Rob's voice, I cashed my check at the bank in Redfern Village and stopped by the Winn-Dixie to pick up some supplies for Fernando. I had no idea what he liked to eat; the way Rea talked, he hardly ate anything. I thought he could use some cans of Vienna sausage and a loaf of French bread and cheese. I bought peanut butter and apple jelly, a box of saltines, plastic knives and forks, paper towels and toilet paper, and a selection of those fruit juices that come in boxes, so they don't have to be refrigerated. At the cashier's line, I also picked up candy bars and cinnamon gum, and I threw in a couple of extra Hershey bars for Dad. Before the cashier finished totaling it all up, I went back for candles and matches and extra batteries for Fernando's radio and a can opener. I couldn't think what else he would need, but it was just as well. My money had almost run out.

Instead of parking near the station, I pulled into a space at the bathhouse by the boardwalk. To avoid suspicion, I walked to the beach first and checked out the scene—a few joggers, a birder with an enormous yellow hat, and a dead ray, washed up and stinking in the sand. The only disquieting note was that I couldn't shake the memory of the stunned look on Rob's face when I had asked how far along Deidre was. I assumed he'd have to tell her. That was part of the revenge. But it hadn't occurred to me how Deidre would react when he told her what I'd said. I suppose it would have occurred to me if I'd been thinking about anybody but myself.

It's true I thought about Fernando constantly, but it was about him in relation to me. And not just because I loved him. Love, after all, what is that? I'm talking about need, about a vacuum that can be filled, in this case by a boy from another country with eyes like volcanic soil, a bad heart, and sorrow literally written into his face.

The joggers had disappeared around the curve past the jetties, and the birder had trained her binoculars out to sea. At last, I felt like the coast was clear. I wandered back toward the Coast Guard station, pretending to examine the brittle sage and liverwort that lined the boardwalk. I stopped at the Jeep to get the sack of groceries, it was heavier than I had remembered, and sauntered around the side of the station, like I was headed leisurely toward one of the beach houses across the dunes. I knocked once on the cellar door, waited, and then knocked again.

The breeze had shifted. It was Gulf Stream air, unseasonably warm and perplexing. I knocked a third time, and the idea seized me that Fernando might have disappeared again. *Búscame en la luz,* I thought. I went to a ground-floor window and peered in. The room was larger and emptier than I had remembered —a few wooden desks, a recruitment calendar on one of the wooden supports, and that nautical map still pinned to the bulletin board. Except for dancing dust motes, that was it.

I sat on the cellar doors until I started to get un-comfortable thinking that somebody might be watch-ing me. After I had knocked a final time and gotten no answer, I walked back to the Jeep. I wasn't pan-icked yet. Fernando had a way of appearing at unex-pected times. It wasn't a good idea for him to be out walking around during daylight, but that was his deci-sion, not mine. I tooled slowly down the streets around East Beach and then Rea's street, on the hunch that he may have gone back to visit her. No one answered her door either, or the door at the top of the stairs.

By the time I got home, I knew Dad would be expecting me to rush off late to the stables again. At some point I'd have to tell him I'd been fired. But not yet. I hid the grocery sack in the garage under a tarp

Dad had used to cover the pit at the Labor Day church barbecue.

Something told me I should go to what we call the front door, the door facing the Marshes of Glynn and far-off Brunswick. But I opened the back door instead, and there in the kitchen on a counter stool sat Fernando, his shirt off and his arms pitifully thin and brown in the harsh fluorescent light. Dad was listening to Fernando's heart by pressing the stethoscope against his back, and I felt like my own heart was going to come out of my chest.

"What's wrong?" I said.

They looked up at me, startled. I glanced at Fernando, then at Dad, then back at Fernando again.

"Fernando's not feeling well," Dad said. "He's running a fever and has had another fainting spell. But he'll be all right, won't you, Fernando? You can put your shirt back on now."

"It's all right," Fernando said to me as he slipped into his shirt. "I'm fine," he said.

"I want to know what's going on," I said.

"I tried to call you at the stables," Dad said. "Mrs. Commodore said you weren't working today."

"That's right. Or tomorrow. Or the day after that. Now somebody tell me what's going on."

Fernando smiled thinly at me. His pupils were contracted against the light.

"Excuse us a moment, Fernando," Dad said and he ushered me into the hall. "Try to keep it together," he whispered. "There's nothing to get panicked about. Fernando's going to need a ride back to wherever he's staying. His temperature's a hundred and three. Take the wagon. I volunteered to give him a ride, but he said he'd rather not let anybody know where he lives. He said you were the only person who knew. Is that right?"

"Yes."

"Then I don't suppose you'd mind taking him?"

"Of course not. I just came from there. I have some groceries and stuff. What's wrong with him?"

Dad had gone into my bathroom and was washing his hands at the sink. "I can't be sure," he said, "but I'm afraid it might be endocarditis, a bacterial infection of the defective valve. I drew some blood to confirm it, but everything is pointing that way. He's even got splinter hemorrhages under his nails."

I shuddered. "Is he going to be all right?"

"I don't know. I've given him a box of samples of amoxicillin, and I'd like you to pick up some Tylenol at the drugstore on your way. I don't know how much good the oral antibiotics will do. He needs them intravenously. I've told him he ought to be in the hospital."

"What'd he say?"

"He's afraid the hospital would call the I.N.S. He says he'll be better in the morning."

"So did you try to talk him into turning himself in?"

Dad turned the water off. There are times when he looks even bigger than he is. "I've been trying to talk him into going to the hospital, April."

Splinter hemorrhages under his nails. I imagined Fernando's fingertips with tiny lines under the nails, like miniature webs or shattered glass. What an odd thing to notice about a person. What an odd thing to be looking for. But then I realized how fixated I was on the details of Fernando's face, the size of his pupils, the angle of his chin, and the point where his scar ended just shy of his temple. Maybe medicine and love were more alike than I'd thought.

All I knew was that I didn't want Fernando to die.

18

Fernando waited in the station wagon while I ran into the drugstore for Tylenol. The line at the cashier was a long one, and I kept glancing out the plate glass window, afraid Fernando would slip away again if I didn't keep an eye on him. When I got back to the wagon, he was sitting up straight.

"I thank you for what you are doing. I am fine now," he said.

"I'm just following doctor's orders. Here. Take two of each of these." I'd broken open the box of amoxicillin and the Tylenol, and I handed him a Coke to wash the pills down. Then I cranked the wagon and eased out into traffic toward the deserted Coast Guard station.

"I think your father has made a decision about me."

"What?"

"I think he wants me to turn myself in to the authorities."

I took a minute to collect myself, because of course that's what I had thought, too. Or at least that's what I had accused Dad of. But the instant the words came from Fernando's mouth instead of my own, I knew they weren't true. "That's what I thought, too," I said, "but I know Dad better than that. He wouldn't lie to you, Fernando. He really wants you to go to the hospital."

"I cannot do that."

"I understand. And I think Dad would, too, if he knew the whole story. He doesn't, does he?"

"I have not told him everything I have told you, but he knows I cannot stay here much longer."

That was not what I wanted to hear.

"Nobody knows where you are," I reminded him. "Rea doesn't even know."

"I do not want her involved any more than she is. She could lose her job. Your father could lose his."

"That leaves me, and I've already lost mine," I said.

He smiled back, and his teeth flashed in the dashboard lights. I was reminded how rarely he smiled, but how special it was when he did.

We parked at the boardwalk to the public beach and waited until the coast was clear. We didn't talk much. Fernando's eyes had a feverish sheen. The clouds were low and pocked, like an upside down egg carton. There wasn't any wind at all, and the people coming back from the beach were dragging their feet in the sand. The only ones who walk on the beach in January are the health nuts or the really lonely—widows and widowers, the newly divorced, or girls who've just broken up with their boyfriends and are going to write poetry about it someday.

When there was no one left to see us, we got out of the wagon and walked to the side of the Coast Guard station. The stairway into the cellar was cold and damp, but the cellar itself, empty as it was, seemed like home. I insisted Fernando lie on the couch. I kissed him on the forehead. His skin was salty and hot.

There was so much I wanted to learn, but I didn't know where to begin. "Tell me this and I won't ask any more about El Salvador," I said.

"What?"

"The night you got the scar. Do you ever feel guilty that you were the one who survived?"

"Yes."

"But you had no control over it."

"No."

"You know that nothing you could have done would have changed the outcome, don't you?"

"Listen, April. I am grateful that I survived. But my gratitude is not perfect or complete. The others died. One of them in the pile with me, a boy named Jorge Ochoa, he squeezed my hand before he died. For this, I will always feel anger and guilt. Always. Who can escape being human? Who would want to? We were meant for this, no? We were not made angels."

"Maybe not, but we were made for something better than what you went through," I said.

"You are right. This is what we were made for." He gestured toward the cellar. "Here we are, you and I. We do not know what will happen. But for this moment, we are together. This is grace. It is a miracle either of us is alive."

Dad had already gone to bed by the time I got back from the Coast Guard station. The Tylenol had brought Fernando's fever down and he had been sleeping peacefully when I left. I turned all the lights on in the kitchen and made a cup of chamomile tea, maybe hoping the sound of the microwave beeper going off would wake Dad up. I wanted him to see that I hadn't stayed out all night with Fernando, and that I was still in one piece. But Dad didn't wake up, and I drank the chamomile in his recliner while I thumbed through a book of photographs of El Salvador, one of the books I'd gotten at the library but hadn't had a chance to look at before.

At first the photos were innocent enough—street scenes in the capital, a first communion, a wedding, and workers picking coffee beans. And then, almost imperceptibly, the photos became darker and more menacing. Soldiers frisking bus passengers and checking for IDs. Demonstrators with their fists raised and kerchiefs covering their faces. Then women looking through photo albums in the office of a human rights commission. The faces in the albums were bloodied and swollen, and I realized the women were looking through the albums for their fathers or sons or brothers. And after that, almost all the photos were of the dead or dying. A man's body being dragged by his feet through the street by soldiers. Two dead women by the side of the road, their hands tied behind their backs and their bare feet splayed outward. The worst, though, was the body dump at a place called El Playon, where a line of vultures looked down on the naked bodies of five men in various stages of decomposition. The bodies were surrounded by the bones of previous victims. The caption said they had been dumped there by death squads.

I don't know what I had expected. I loved Fernando, I really did, but for an instant I was angry at him for bringing his world, so full of darkness and chaos, into mine. Before I'd met him, I hadn't even known where El Salvador was. Now I had heard and seen things about it I would never forget, even if I tried. I closed the book. I held it to my chest. I felt like a fool for thinking he had come from paradise.

The next morning I got up and ran a brush through my hair. I normally go to the bathroom and brush my teeth first thing, but I was putting off going into the hall. I didn't want to run into Dad. I knew I didn't have anything to feel guilty about, but I felt vaguely guilty anyway.

He knocked on the door. "You awake, April?"

"Yeah, but I'm not dressed."

"That's okay. I just wanted you to know there's someone here, so you wouldn't be alarmed."

I stepped closer to the door. "Who is it?" I said.

"Our friend from the I.N.S. No reason to hurry."

"I'll be out in a minute," I said. I flung my brush onto the bed.

I took my time in the shower and dressed in my most faded pair of blue jeans and a tie-dyed orange and yellow T-shirt, my hair pulled into a ponytail so tight my eyebrows were nearly stretched all the way to my ears.

Dad and Mr. Blake were glued to the morning news show, and when Blake started to get up from the sofa, I waved him back down again. He was wearing that same baggy brown sweater despite the fact that it was going to be unseasonably hot. When he smiled up at me, his teeth were yellow in the morning light off the marsh.

"Mr. Blake brought a packet of information for you," Dad said as he turned off the TV. On the coffee table was a blue folder, with an official looking emblem on the front, an eagle and all that.

"Thanks," I said. "You could have just mailed it."

"It was on my way," Blake said. "Besides, I thought of a few other things I wanted to ask your dad."

"There's toast and jelly in the kitchen, Mrs. Silkin's pear preserves," Dad reminded me.

"I'll get some on the way out," I said, and I pulled up this huge, stuffed footstool Dad had brought from Atlanta and sat on it, midway between the two men.

Mr. Blake continued to smile at me. "I was just explaining to your father why the Service is so interested in Salvadoran refugees."

I looked from one to the other. Dad's face was blank. Mr. Blake's was irritatingly friendly. "So what makes you so interested in Salvadoran refugees?" I asked.

Blake turned fully toward me. His legs were crossed at the knee. "I'm looking for a particular boy, April. He's about your age, maybe a little older. He's from a town called El Paraíso, in the northern part of El Salvador, where the fighting has been the heaviest."

I had to count the hairs on Blake's nose to keep my chin from shaking.

"This boy worked at the local army garrison, in the foreign officers' billet, because of his excellent English, which he had learned from missionaries. We've been told he was a bright young man, but quiet and a bit mysterious."

I cocked my head and glanced out the window. I pretended to be watching the birds.

"Last June the guerrillas launched a surprise attack against the garrison," Blake said. "More than two hundred soldiers were killed, including several American military advisors, one from Georgia as a matter of fact. After the attack, the boy I've been telling you about disappeared."

I glanced back at him. "I'm having trouble following you," I said honestly.

"I'll keep it brief," Blake replied. "We think the

160

boy was actually a guerrilla who passed information to his commanders about security weaknesses inside the garrison."

"A spy," Dad said.

"A terrorist," Blake added.

I leaned forward, my elbows on my knees. "That's interesting," I said. "But what if the boy disappeared only because he was scared?"

"Scared of what?" Blake said. "If you haven't done anything wrong, you don't have anything to fear."

"In America, maybe that's true," I said. "It's supposed to be true, anyway. But maybe in El Salvador, that's not the way things work."

"You've been reading up on El Salvador then," Blake said with a satisfied grin.

I swallowed. "A little. I don't know much, but I do know that in El Salvador things are sometimes not what they seem. Maybe this boy you're talking about hadn't done anything wrong, but maybe he was tortured by the military and left for dead, and that's why he never came back. Isn't that a possibility?" I said.

"Anything is possible, but that's for a court to decide."

"Illegal aliens aren't entitled to due process," I said.

"Very good, April. You're right. I was thinking of a Salvadoran court."

"Oh. Right," I said. "There's justice for you."

Blake took a deep breath. "Look, April. There's no point in us beating around the bush with each other. Do you know the boy I'm talking about? His name's Fernando Ramirez."

I didn't say anything.

"I'd prefer you ask me those kinds of questions," Dad said.

"I already have, haven't I, Dr. Hunter?" Blake got up. He buttoned his sweater all the way up and looked around, as if for a hat, although he hadn't been wearing one. Then he stopped in his tracks and looked again at Dad and me. "You're very nice people, but let me tell you something. Americans don't give a flit about El Salvador," he said. "It's too complicated, too foreign, too small. But Americans care about their young men getting killed. It doesn't matter where. And I don't think there would be a lot of sympathy for people who are trying to hide an alien who might have been involved in the murder of American soldiers."

There was a long silence then. Dad and I didn't look at each other, but I could feel him bristling even more than before. Mr. Blake must have finally understood that he was no longer welcome, because he thanked Dad for the coffee, and me for the company, and had almost made it to the door before he turned back to us.

"You've got a lot going for you right now, Dr. Hunter. I'd hate to see it all go up in smoke."

"I appreciate your concern," Dad said, "but I don't think you have to worry. We'll get along just fine."

Blake smiled his tight-lipped smile and nodded

good-bye toward me. Then he was gone. I heard his feet rustling in the live oak leaves. They fall at different times, just about all through the year, so there're always dead leaves around, even after the flowers begin to bloom.

"How's Fernando doing?" Dad asked a moment later as we stood in the kitchen, watching Blake's beige pickup pull into traffic on the Sea Island Road.

"His fever was down when I left," I said. "He'd started the antibiotics."

Dad turned around to face me. "I guess you still don't want to tell me where he is."

I shook my head. I had wanted to see Fernando on my way to school, but I was afraid Blake or one of his men might try to follow me. "I'll check on him this afternoon and let you know what's up."

Dad put his hands on my shoulders. "When you go to see him, keep your eyes open, you know what I mean? And give me a call at the hospital," he said. "I'll be there until ten."

I glanced into his face and thought I saw the seed of something fragile and good pushing to the surface. I wondered if he saw the same thing in me.

19

I was sick with worry about Fernando, but I felt like I couldn't run the risk of leading the I.N.S. to him, so I went on to school. In retrospect, that was the third mistake I made.

When I pulled into the parking lot at the academy, the only vacant space was next to Rob Allard's classic Corvette. I'd never taken a close look at it before. He must have saved it from being cannibalized by not more than a few minutes. It was taped all up and smeared with something they call Bondo, and to tell you the truth I never would have recognized it as a Corvette or anything else, it looked so mummified. He and Deidre were in the carcass, the windows rolled up, but I could tell Rob saw me despite his sunglasses and I lip-read him saying, "Speak of the devil."

Deidre didn't turn around. That should have given it away that she was mad. But my mind was on

Fernando, so I didn't *see* Deidre not wanting to see me.

I closed the Jeep door, slung my backpack over a shoulder and pushed my sunglasses up on my nose. It was terrible weather, warm and humid, and still in a way that January air should never be still. Mr. Noonan was outside by the incinerator smoking a cigarette. I'm sure this was not school policy, although we all knew a few teachers still smoked in the lounge despite the no smoking signs. Noonan arched one of his eyebrows in a kind of greeting. I'm glad he was wearing tinted glasses. I didn't have to see the look in his eye as I passed. I am honestly not attracted to teachers in the way some students seem to be. I pity them, the teachers I mean, they seem so stuck in the middle of their lives and miserable there.

"April?" Noonan said, and I turned and forced a smile as though I hadn't really seen him yet.

He put out the butt of his cigarette on the bottom of his shoe and then tucked in his shirt a little at the belt. "Have I ever told you that you intrigue me?" he said.

"No." And I wanted to add: Please don't break your streak.

"Who do you have first period?"

"Garner, trig, I still don't know what it is." I had started walking, and Noonan was walking beside me, past the monument to the four Brunswick firemen who had died when the roof of the original academy fell in on them at the turn of the century. The monument was an urn shaped like an angel's wing.

"I never did understand trig, either," he said. His hands were in his pockets. He smelled like nicotine and an off-brand cologne. A vandal had painted SUCK ONE! on the steps leading to the main building, and I felt like we were both pretending not to notice. Inside, I took off my shades.

"Your eyes are blue," Noonan said in mock alarm. "For some reason I had them pictured green."

"Huh." I had stopped outside the women's bathroom, and I was just about to excuse myself and go in, when Noonan did something unexpected. He took my journal out of this folder he was carrying in his hand.

"Where'd you get that?" I asked.

"You left it on your desk after our free writing period last week."

"I'm glad you found it," I said. "Thanks." But it bothered me that he'd had it all week without saying anything.

"You have genuine promise as a writer," he began, but he didn't have to. I knew in an instant that he'd read the whole thing.

"You don't have children, do you?" I asked.

He shook his head.

"That's good." I hadn't exactly meant it as an insult, but he must have taken it that way when I snatched the journal out of his hand and walked into the bathroom. I could have stiff-armed somebody if I'd needed to. But the only person in the bathroom was Deidre Holloway, who saw me coming in the

166

mirror and left in a swirl of lilac perfume without even turning the water off in the sink.

I can't be held accountable for everybody's unhappiness, I decided. I was unhappy enough myself as it was. So Noonan was a voyeur and probably needed to see a shrink. Who didn't? And Deidre wasn't speaking to me because I'd asked Rob Allard how far along she was. I'd screwed up, I admit it, like most people do when they try to get revenge, but so be it. I wouldn't be around the island much longer anyway. I had this vision of Fernando and me in my old red Jeep heading south, through Port Arthur and Brownsville and all of dusty Mexico, through Guatemala and Honduras, and into the mountains to the white-stuccoed walls of El Paraíso.

The thought of Fernando kept me buoyed up during trig and an otherwise insufferable lecture in history, something about Dred Scott. I ate lunch alone near the window, looking out over what struck me now as a hopelessly provincial town. The last classes, including advanced lit, didn't break my spirit because Fernando was waiting for me at the deserted Coast Guard station, sick but ultimately recoverable. When the final bell rang, I didn't look to the right or left, but headed straight as a shot for the parking lot. Cranking the Jeep and turning onto the boulevard, I felt like my life was just beginning to open up.

Once on the island, I stopped again at the Winn-Dixie for a few things, including a pint of fudge ripple ice cream for Fernando, and got stuck in the longest line I'd ever seen there. "What's the crowd about?" I asked the woman in front of me, a bleached blonde in cutoffs and a Curious George sweatshirt. Her two-year-old clung to her like a secondary appendage.

"Double coupons," she said.

"Huh."

So the line moved like molasses, and some of the women shrieked when they saw somebody in line they knew. The friends would hug for a long time and then comment on each other's hair and ask about the kids.

"I normally go to the Food Fair in Brunswick," the woman in front of me said, "but I figure I couldn't pass this up." After paying for my stuff, I helped her out with her groceries, and just as we reached her car, a little Toyota hatchback, horns started blaring and people began running across the parking lot toward the intersection in front of Hardee's, where a minor fender bender had occurred. The wind had picked up, and the air was sticky and hot.

"It's been such a hard winter," the woman began as I put the last of her groceries in the trunk—something about her best friend and her ex-husband and child support checks that might never come—and it literally took me half an hour to get away from her.

By the time I did, it was almost dark. The streetlights were on, and I was sure the fudge ripple ice cream had melted, but I figured when I got to the Coast Guard station, I could do an amusing imitation for Fernando of the woman in the Curious George sweatshirt.

Then it seized me that Fernando probably thought I wasn't going to show up at all. Instead of parking near the boardwalk to the beach and working my way back over the dunes to avoid attracting attention, I headed straight for the station. The Jeep slung gravel against the Dempsey Dumpster as I pulled into the empty parking lot.

The cellar door was ajar, but I knocked anyway. There was no answer. I opened the door and clicked on my flashlight. "Fernando?" I whispered. The steps led down into darkness, and if there had been an answer then, I wouldn't have heard it. The wind behind me had gusted, sending a metal garbage can clattering down the driveway of the nearest beach house. The trees along the road were groaning.

I knew as I descended the stairs that something wasn't right, even before my flashlight played across the empty couch, its blanket kicked onto the floor. The building seemed to shimmy. Outside I heard the sound of snapping wood. Upstairs glass shattered. But I stood rooted to the spot where I'd dropped my flashlight. I was looking down at Fernando, who was staring up at me from the floor in a pool of light. His eyes were half-lidded, his mouth slightly opened. He did not respond when I said his name or when I shook him gently by the shoulders. The way his head wobbled frightened me. I thought he was either dead or dying, and I didn't know what to do. I accidentally kicked the flashlight when I stood up. It rolled under the couch, so I had to grope my way back up the stairs in darkness and out into the tail end of the storm.

20

The streetlights were out as far as I could see, the roofs of the dark houses silhouetted against a racing sky the color of zinc. You can't believe how dark it is on the island without power. I might as well have been in Siberia or on one of Saturn's moons. Dad had figured out how to get the Jeep's top up, but it had a leak. When I started the engine, a stream of icy water ran down my back, but I hardly felt it. I was in a panic about Fernando. And I hadn't driven three blocks past the intersection of Demere and Frederica when I came up against the first of the downed live oaks. There was no way around it. It was like the fuselage of a medium-sized plane. I backed up, turned around, and saw smaller trees lying in yards all along the way, some across the hoods and roofs of parked cars or blocking sidewalks and driveways.

After the intersection, the road to Fort Frederica was clear except for limbs and branches small enough for the Jeep to negotiate in four wheel drive. I turned at the stables. The live oak in the center of the ring was down. It had splintered a section of the fence, but at least it had fallen toward the road instead of the stables where the horses, drowsing, would have been crushed to death. I slid into my customary parking place by the lunging pit.

The sky had cleared momentarily. I saw or felt the light from a full moon. It made my fumbling with the lock less protracted, and filled the inside of the barn with a platinum glow. Down the aisle I could see Trader alert and waiting at the door of his stall, as though he had been expecting to find me at the center of this catastrophe, but I didn't have time for him. I had only come to try the phone on the counter by the insurance forms, to call Dad and tell him to get to the Coast Guard station as fast as he could, but the phone was dead. In the dark I could feel the pounding of my heart.

Suddenly I was conscious of a faint bubbling noise. I went to the door of Mrs. Commodore's office, where a light cast shadows on the ceiling. Behind her desk sat Mr. Commodore in his wheelchair, his portable breathing machine making a sound like an aquarium. A flashlight was askew in his lap, pointing crazily up into his face. His eyes were as translucent as a fish's belly, and he was holding a portable radio to his ear.

"Phone's dead in here, too," he said. "Whole island's cut off." He lowered the radio.

"It's an emergency," I said. "I've got to get to Brunswick." I headed for the door.

"The causeway's blocked," he said, and I stopped in my tracks. "Tractor trailer rig overturned in the wind."

I looked at him.

"There are power outages as far away as Jesup," he continued. "You're Mad Jack Hunter's daughter, aren't you?"

"His name's just Jack."

"I'm sorry. I didn't mean anything by that. What's the emergency?"

"A friend of mine is sick."

"A foreigner?"

The word cut.

"I've got to go."

"April?" he said. I turned back around.

"Your name is April, isn't it?"

"Yes, my name is April."

He nodded and then said, "Take care."

It was like I was hearing the words for the first time.

"What?" I asked.

"Take care," he said again.

"Oh. Sure. Thanks." But for the first time it meant something to me as I headed back out into the night.

I jumped into the Jeep and turned the key, but the engine wouldn't start. I took my foot off the accelerator and tried again. The battery was strong, but the

Jeep wouldn't crank. I counted to five, hoping the engine was just flooded, but I had a feeling water had probably gotten in and shorted something out. When it didn't start the fourth time, I got out again and slammed the door shut. I didn't know what I was going to do. I was just standing in the rain paralyzed by fear and indecision, when a car's headlights approached on the Fort Frederica Road. I couldn't believe it when the car turned at the stables and pulled into the space next to mine by the lunging pit. It was Rob Allard's classic Corvette.

I opened the passenger door before it had come to a complete stop.

"Hey!" Rob said. "What do you think you're doing?"

I got in. "Just drive. I've got to get to Brunswick."

"Brunswick? Dream on. The causeway's out."

"I don't care. Just go."

"No way."

"Go. *Go*."

"You're soaking wet. You're dripping on everything. Get out of here. I've got to check on Mr. Commodore."

"He's fine." I grabbed for the gearshift.

Rob intercepted my hand and squeezed it hard, staring me straight in the eye. He had on an Atlanta Braves cap and his worn-out leather aviator's jacket. There was bad blood between us but I couldn't afford a grudge now, and whatever he saw in my eyes convinced him he couldn't afford one, either. He let my hand go. "All right," he said. "All right. But there better be a good reason for this." He cut his wheels and jerked the gearshift into reverse. When his foot came off the clutch into first, the car lurched ahead, peeling rubber when the tires hit the asphalt of the road.

We sped along Sea Island Road past the marsh until we came to our house, the house shaped like a bird, and I saw that the oak by the garage had fallen neatly into the very center of the roof, scattering the Spanish tile and exposing the beams of the great room. With Dad at the hospital, I didn't have anything in there I couldn't afford to lose. I felt bad for Dad, though. He was so proud of the place he'd made for us there.

Rob was furious, but that was okay. It just made him drive faster. At the entrance to the causeway, though, he slowed, and I saw what Mr. Commodore had been talking about—barricades, a cluster of police cars, spotlights, and two wreckers. A blue and white tractor trailer rig had jackknifed across three lanes. "Keep going," I said.

"Bullshit."

"Somebody's life's at stake."

"Tell *them* about it." He jerked his head toward the flashing cop cars.

"I can't."

"Great."

I put my hand on his forearm. "Please help me, Rob," I said, as evenly as I could.

He looked at me again. He must have known

175

how serious I was. He eased the Corvette forward until a cop stopped him. A guy in a yellow hardhat was moving one of the barricades so that a power company truck could get through. The cop waved Rob away with a circular motion. Turn around and go back, his hands said. Rob pretended not to understand. He continued to inch forward.

"Hey, you!" the cop shouted. "Road's closed! You blind or something?"

Rob smiled and nodded, but just kept going. I could tell he was starting to get into this. He had always been good at playing dumb. I tried to stare straight ahead, but out of the corner of my eye, I saw the cop's face blanch as we slowly passed him. Rob nonchalantly wound around the jackknifed truck and the power crew and a pair of startled firemen with disheveled hair. My pulse was racing in my neck as he shifted into third, picked up speed, and looked up to watch the flashing lights recede in his rearview mirror. The causeway ahead of us was absolutely empty and dark, and I felt like we were convicts on the run.

"So," he said, "is this how you've been getting your rocks off lately?"

I didn't say anything. On either side I could see the silver marsh and the distant lights of Brunswick, where the power had not been disrupted.

"Every cop on the island knows my car," he said. He took off his baseball cap and flipped it into the back. "It's your friend from South America, isn't it?" he said. I didn't correct him.

He was silent for a minute. "I'm gonna go there

one day," he finally said. "My recruiter says I'll be able to travel military anywhere in the world real cheap."

The rivers passed beneath us one by one, the Frederica, the MacKay, the Little, and the Back.

"Of course, I'm not going to make a career of it," he said. "Just enough to where they'll pay for college. If I can get into college. I mean, college isn't everything."

The last river was wide, smooth, and undisturbed. The moon moved in and out behind those high, metallic clouds, and occasionally I could see it reflected in the water below. Rob just kept on talking. I was grateful he hadn't asked a lot of questions. I thought about what it would be like to reach for the moon on the water, the way it would feel when the image fell apart in my hands.

That was my life, I thought. And hadn't it always been like me to take the wrong way to get where I had to go, and to persevere in it out of some kind of crooked stubbornness. I wanted to blame everything on Dad, who had turned my childhood into a maze, or on my mother. She had given in to him, coddled him, reassured him that nothing was his fault, that he was simply misunderstood and overworked. Then she turned on me to straighten things out, to clean up after the party had turned sour, to explain the broken glass to the neighbors, and put out the smoldering mattress Dad had hauled out onto the front lawn. But now I saw that I had been so addicted to the mess I'd grown up in, I couldn't leave it behind. I'd brought it to the island, thinking I was escaping it when really I was only transplanting it. It really didn't matter that Dad had sobered up and started a new life, because I hadn't. I was addicted to turmoil, and that was what Fernando had supplied for me. Maybe that's why I had fallen in love with him.

"I'm sorry about the way I've been," I suddenly said to Rob.

"Huh?"

"I'm sorry, Rob. I really am."

He knew what I was talking about. "That's okay," he said. "But Deidre's the one you ought to say that to."

"I know. I wanted to pay you back."

"For what?"

"For getting me fired."

Rob glanced over at me. "I wasn't the one who did that," he said. He looked back at the road. "But I can see why you thought I was."

He slowed as we got to the Brunswick end of the causeway. I figured the cop had radioed ahead, and that there'd be police cars waiting for us on the mainland, their weapons drawn. But of course there weren't. The traffic light at the intersection was blinking yellow on one side and red on the other. Cars were out. The streets were brightly lit. It was like nothing out of the ordinary had happened that night. The storm had been on the island, not here. For a minute I forgot where I was going and why. And then I had this picture of Fernando in my head, staring up at me in the pool of light.

"Get to the hospital as fast as you can."

Rob floored it around the curve and took a back way that only the kids who'd grown up there knew. When he pulled up at the emergency entrance, I said, "Thanks." I got out without another word and walked straight in. I didn't stop when they asked me to fill out a patient information form. I didn't stop when an orderly told me I couldn't go through that door at the end of the hall. I looked in the examination rooms as I passed. The patients were too scared or hurting to be startled. The nurses didn't bat an eye.

I went up the back stairwell to the lobby, taking the steps two at a time. The volunteer at the information desk didn't have a clue who my father was or where he might be. I was staring at the mouse pin on her lapel as I backed away and so didn't see Dad feeding quarters into the juice machine by the closed gift shop until he had said, "April? What's the matter? What's wrong?"

He didn't look good in the harsh fluorescent light. He had circles under his eyes, and his tunic was rumpled and stained. But he was my father, and I think I fully understood in that moment that he had always been.

"It's Fernando," I said.

When Dad and I screeched up to the Coast Guard station that night in the station wagon, I was preparing myself for the worst. I was sure that Fernando had died and that it had been my fault because I hadn't taken care of him, hadn't known what to do when I saw him lying on the floor. I almost didn't go down the steps into the cellar with Dad, but at the last minute I followed him down. At the bottom of the steps, the light from Dad's emergency lantern fell across an empty floor. Fernando had disappeared.

If it hadn't been for that change of clothes still folded neatly on the couch beside his radio and books —a New Testament, a boy's collection of adventure stories, and a well-used guide to the island—I might have started doubting that he had really been there at all. We gave each floor a quick check. No sign of him. At first I was ecstatic, of course, because he hadn't died, but then I felt foolish for all the trouble I'd caused Dad. He told me it would have been foolish *not* to come get him. Fernando was obviously very sick. Then I really started worrying about where Fernando might be. Dad checked the men's bathhouse at the beach, and I combed the station again with the emergency lantern. Together we walked the dunes in a widening circle around the station. The moon helped, but the island still looked stricken and remote without electricity, and we didn't go far before we turned back.

At the station again, Dad made me repeat everything I'd told him—about finding Fernando on the floor with his eyes half open, his mouth slack, unresponsive when I tried to talk to him, even when I shook him. "But he was breathing, wasn't he?" Dad asked, and all I could say was, "I don't know." It's maddening how little attention you pay even in an emergency. I had just got it in my head that he was dying or dead, and I took off into the tail end of the storm without making sure either way.

"It's an odd thing," Dad said. He was sitting on the upturned Coke box in the control room at the top of the station. "If his fever had spiked high enough, I suppose he could have had a febrile seizure, although we wouldn't expect to see that in someone his age."

Then a terrible thought hit me. "Maybe somebody came and got him."

"I'd thought of that," Dad said, "but it doesn't seem likely, does it?"

I shrugged. "They could have been watching me."

We finally decided that Dad would give me a ride to the village, which hadn't been touched by the storm. Power had already been restored there. He'd go back and start from the station. We'd meet halfway on the beach.

At the village, life seemed normal. Kids were skateboarding in front of the hardware store, the yogurt shop was packed. Out on the pier, couples held hands and watched the lights of Jekyll Island. I continued to ask around, but nobody had seen a thin, dark stranger. When I mentioned the scar, they looked like they didn't believe me.

I hung around the playground for a little while, chatting with the mothers about their children and then gradually working into a conversation about Fernando. The name mystified them. He couldn't be from around here, their eyes seemed to say.

It was pitch black and cold when I gave up and headed back along the beach. When I reached the rock jetties, where the beach curved toward the deserted Coast Guard station, I felt the presence of someone else nearby. I looked up at the silhouette on the rocks, praying it was Fernando, but even at that distance I knew it was Rea Britt.

"Terrible storm," she said when I got to her.

"Fernando's gone again."

"That's what Jack tells me. Where have you been looking?"

"The village."

"Find out anything?"

"Nobody's seen him. Some of them don't even act like they know we've had a storm."

"Stores open?"

I nodded.

"Hmm," she said.

"What are you doing out here?" I asked as I sat on a rock beside her.

Rea glanced at the lighthouse and then back toward the beach. "Do you know any Spanish?"

"I'm learning a little."

"Then you may know what this means: *'Búscame en la luz.'*"

It startled me at first, until I remembered that Fernando had left a note for her, too. "I know what it means, and this is the right place," I said. "But I don't think he's going to show up here."

"I don't either. Maybe he will tomorrow night."

Then we sat in silence for a while, the surest sign that, despite our difference in age, we were friends.

"I asked Jack if you two would like to stay at my house until your roof's fixed," Rea finally said. "I can't stand for that room upstairs to go vacant."

"Why?"

"I don't know. I guess it's tied up with my mother."

I didn't ask anything else, because I wasn't sure I wanted to hear about Rea's mother, but she didn't need any more questions to keep her going. All she needed was the dark and someone sitting in it with her who had ears.

"I made a conscious decision one time that I've regretted," she said. "Mother was dying of cancer. Nobody knew for sure how long she had. One doctor said three months. Another said she could last two years. All I knew was that the end was coming. I also knew I was going to have to stop drinking. Mother had been after me about it for years. I'd hit bottom the summer before, right before she moved in. I won't go into details. You know the score. I knew I had to stop. I knew I was *going* to stop. But I didn't. I waited for Mother to die. I knew at the time what I was doing, and I did it anyway. I didn't want my mother to have the satisfaction of seeing me sober before she died. That's how low I had sunk."

I waited for more of the story, but there wasn't any.

"Sobriety is a two-edged sword," Rea finally said.

"Unless you're sober, you don't have to face up to things like that."

"But she knew you loved her," I said.

Rea didn't answer, and I realized the question was beside the point.

"Look," I said. "There's something I've got to get straight with you. I never had a twin. I made that story up. I don't know why. I'm sorry."

"I understand," she said, as if she'd known all along it was a lie. "Whatever made you think of twins?"

The beam from the lighthouse swung around. It did not hurt to look at it. For a light that can be seen all those miles at sea, it is surprisingly weak close up and head on. The light touched the buoy at the head of the sound, the crests of the waves closer in, and finally something nearly erect on the beach that cast a long, pale shadow in the sand. It was Dad. He was moving slowly and awkwardly from left to right, a big, complicated mammal that might have wandered just that moment out of the sea.

"Sometimes I wonder whether I really love Dad," I said to Rea. "I mean, I knew how to love him when he was drunk. I had so much practice at that. But this is different."

Rea nodded. "Jack!" she called. "We're up here! Jack!"

He squinted against the light and gave us a clumsy wave before the beam of the lighthouse moved on and plunged him into darkness again.

"I'm the last person in the world to give advice

about love," Rea said. "But somebody once told me that you ought to start low, with somebody you couldn't possibly hope to love, and then work your way up."

At first, I thought of Rob Allard, but then I realized I'd have to start even lower than that. I'd have to start with myself.

21

Fernando didn't show up the next day, or the next. After considerable thought, and against what he said was his better judgment, Dad reported him missing to the St. Simons police and the Georgia Bureau of Investigation. He called the local office of the I.N.S., but they wouldn't answer any questions, referring him instead to a spokesman in Washington, who would not even confirm or deny that someone named Blake worked for them. As for this Salvadoran refugee named Fernando Ramirez, were we family? "No," Dad said. "Friends." In any case, the spokesman said, there's no way to check and see if he's under custody unless you give an identification number. Every alien under federal custody has an identification number. "How would we know his number if we don't even know whether you've got him?" The spokesman said he couldn't help us there. Dad argued with him a minute, and then slammed the phone down so hard it cracked the receiver.

Dad felt bad about that. It was Rea's phone.

It took that day or two before I realized something else was wrong. My Jeep. The night of the storm, I'd left it at the stables after it wouldn't start. In the turmoil of Fernando's disappearance and moving in with Rea, I'd forgotten all about the Jeep until that Sunday afternoon, when I realized I'd need it for school the next day. Dad and Rea had gone to their A.A. meetings. I rode my bicycle to the stables to see if I could get the Jeep cranked. It wasn't there.

At first, I figured Dad must have had it towed in to be repaired, but I later found out he hadn't. Somebody had taken it. Of course, the first person who sprang to mind was Fernando. But I just couldn't believe he'd do something like that. I chalked it up to kids taking advantage of the storm to go for a joy ride. We reported the theft to the police, and figured the Jeep would turn up on the island soon, abandoned. We just hoped it would be in decent shape.

It didn't, though. The days stretched into weeks. Deidre continued to avoid me, and I felt like I had no friends at all. I thought all kinds of things, even about moving back to Atlanta, but I put that out of mind after Mother called from Spain to check on me— she'd met an Emory engineering professor (fluid mechanics) who was studying in Madrid on a Fulbright, and she'd decided to stay on in Spain a few more months, maybe because of him. It was useless to even begin to explain to her about Fernando—I knew I'd tell her everything when she got back to the states, but I just couldn't get into it all then—so I just kept my end of the call cheerful, and asked at the end if she wanted to talk to Dad.

"Maybe another time," she said. "Bye now."

It's hard to describe what I was feeling about Fernando. At first I didn't cry much because I was so busy looking for him, but after a few days, I'd come in from school and go straight to my bed and just lie there sobbing with the pillow over my head. Then later on, I'd forget about him entirely, until something would remind me, like the azaleas coming out, and then the pain was unbearable. Everything that bloomed was a reminder of Fernando, and I thought because of him I'd always hate spring. The feeling was like grief, as though Fernando had died. Maybe he had. That was the thing. I thought I'd never know what had become of him.

And I'd only known him a few weeks. What if he'd been my brother or my father? What if I'd been married to him, had children by him? What if he'd been my son? And what if he'd disappeared like that? Just gone. No word. Ever. How can such a thing be endured?

Rea had given me a photo of Fernando, one of only two she had. It was not flattering, but it was him all right, looking spooked in front of her mantel, with the glare from her camera's flash in the mirror behind him. I had it blown up on leaflets that I posted in the halls at school and on telephone poles in the village and on the road to Fort Frederica: *"¡Desaparecido!"* it said. And underneath: "Disappeared!" Followed by his name, age, and when and where he'd last been seen. "If you have information . . ." it said, and it gave our phone number, but all we got were crank calls, and complaints from the local beautification board. But still, it was reason for hope.

On the last day of class before spring break, school dismissed early for a tree planting ceremony on the front lawn. It was a white oak, to be planted near the memorial to the four firemen, so it would shade the stone angel's wing, I guess. The Peace Oak, it was going to be called. Our principal, a former nurse who had served in Vietnam and didn't normally have much to say, led the procession from the gym, where we'd all been assembled waiting for the school board president and other dignitaries to arrive, including Max Spellmann, the sporting goods magnate, who had given the school its new basketball floor and exhaust fans for the cafeteria. It was one of those days that makes your heart ache for something you can't quite name. High white clouds, a bite of unseasonable cold to the air, and sunlight like the gold filigree on a china bowl. It's the kind of day when you think you might find whatever it is you've lost.

Mr. Noonan followed the dignitaries into a loose semicircle around the spot where the hole had already been partially dug. His mustache needed trimming, and he was wearing a silly vest with medals. Maybe he'd mentioned in class that he'd been in the military, but it hadn't registered on me until then.

I was toward the middle of the crowd of students and so couldn't hear all the speeches. I'm sure I didn't miss much. The only one I paid attention to was our principal's. It was short and to the point. "When you come back to the place where you went to school," she said, "you'll see this tree has grown and you'll think back to this day and remember how good it felt to be alive and young."

The dignitaries looked a little embarrassed by the paucity of what she'd said, but Mr. Noonan began applauding slowly, which started some of the students doing the same. Some other kids, though, were horsing around in the parking lot, and the sounds of their laughter drifted across to us on the cool breeze. The first shovel of dirt was lifted by Rose Grierson, secretary of the student body, who also happened to be an ROTC sponsor and so was in uniform. She had the thickest, blackest hair you are likely to see on a living person. Then came Buddy Ozark, All-State tackle and National Merit Scholar, and Freddie Ferguson, who was a nephew of the school board president. Mr. Noonan helped with the tree itself. The band, not in uniform, struck up "America the Beautiful," which wavered on the breeze like a sad love song, and when it ended the dignitaries left the filling in of the hole to the school's two maintenance men.

But nothing could take the edge off the fragile hope I was feeling, not even the sight of Rob Allard slouched back against the building, his thumbs hooked into the belt loops of his jeans and his denim jacket unbuttoned, revealing a skateboarding T-shirt that nobody but Rob Allard could possibly consider cool. Even his sunglasses were the wrong kind, fluorescent pink, with a chartreuse cord, two years out of synch. I didn't see Deidre until she was right up on me. She had on a denim jacket like Rob's and an oversized shirt with tiny red teddy bears on it.

"Hi," she said, as though her coming up to me were the most natural thing in the world.

I nodded. I was, as they say, struck speechless.

"I told my dad about your friend from El Salvador," she said.

"Your dad?"

"He works at FLETC." The Federal Law Enforcement Training Center. Yes.

A freshman ran between us, shouting an obscenity to a jerk friend of his in the parking lot. When Deidre looked back at me, her hair fell across her face like a veil. It had the texture of spun sunlight, if there could ever be such a thing. I knew then what every boyfriend she'd had must have seen in her—a lightness and softness that he thought could never backfire on him. She could take it. That's what Rob Allard must have thought. She could handle it. I bet up until the minute he proposed, he'd been thinking she was the kind of girl he could make a clean break from. Then right at the last minute, he must have freaked at the thought of losing her, or maybe he'd known all along that she was more than he would ever deserve in life and that he'd be lucky if she even listened long enough for him to say it. I felt like a boy in her presence that day, hurting with love for her even before she said what she had tracked me down in the crowd to say.

"Don't ever tell anyone I told you this," she said. "The government doesn't have your friend. The I.N.S., the F.B.I., they don't know what happened to him any more than you do. My dad ran a computer check. But if anyone found out Dad told me, or I told you, he'd lose his job."

"Oh, Deidre. I understand," I said before I hugged her. It was not the news I had hoped for, but it eliminated one of the possibilities we'd feared. The best thing, though, was that my sometimes friend Deidre had come back to me. So this, I thought, is what forgiveness is.

22

Mrs. Commodore hired me back at the stables after spring break. She said she needed somebody to take care of Trader as he entered middle age. I think she just needed somebody to talk to. I know I did. I told her all about Fernando, and she was sympathetic to a degree. But it's hard, I think, for anybody to understand how a boy who's in your life for such a short time can literally change everything.

It was not long after school started back that Dad got a call from the Savannah police department. Savannah is an old port city about sixty miles north of Brunswick. My Jeep had been found abandoned there at the end of River Street by the docks. I told Dad I just wanted to take a bus to Savannah and drive the Jeep home if it was drivable. The police said it looked like it was in pretty good shape. But Dad wanted to check the Jeep out first. I agreed that was a good idea. Instead of trying to take care of him all the time, I was beginning to let myself depend on him.

We drove into Savannah under palmetto trees and a high, dry wind. After St. Simons, Savannah looked almost third world, with narrow streets and houses with unpainted shutters, graffiti scrawled on the walls. There was a restless, sexy energy there. It occurred to me it wouldn't be such a bad place to live, after college. I'd decided to go to Emory in the fall and major in international relations. I'd live at home with Mother for a while, until I made friends and could get an apartment near campus. Leaving Dad would be hard, but knowing he had Rea Britt for a friend helped. Maybe there would be romance in their future. Or maybe they were simply meant to give each other hope.

We were afraid we couldn't find the address where the Jeep was parked, but it ended up being the most touristy part of the city, a parking lot across from a row of shops and restaurants carved out of the decaying riverfront. The Jeep was parked facing the docks under a sign advertising condominiums with a view. To tell you the truth, I wouldn't have recognized the Jeep. It had been washed and waxed. The top gleamed black in the morning sun.

"They said the key was in the ignition," Dad said. "I told them to leave it there." He parked and we got out of the station wagon. The breeze had picked up and was blowing Dad's thinning hair. He'd started wearing baseball caps, but he'd forgotten to bring one along.

"It looks all right to me," I said.

"All right isn't the word," he said. "Maybe we should get somebody to steal the wagon, too." It was a lame joke, but I smiled anyway.

"There's no need to stick around," I said. "I'll see you at home."

He continued to walk around the Jeep, looking at the tires. "I want to wait and make sure you get it started," he said. "We don't know how long it's been sitting here. The battery might be dead."

He had a point. I opened the door and eased into the driver's seat. The vinyl had been washed and the ashtray emptied of all my chewing gum wrappers. The windshield was so clean it was nearly invisible. The shine on the door handles looked painted on.

The engine started on the first crank. I smiled and waved Dad on.

I thought about Fernando. Maybe he'd gone back to El Salvador, I reasoned. The war there had just ended. I was starting to understand the El Salvadors of the world. Fernando had been a door for me. Before I met him, I'd led such an insular life. I'd always been turned inward, self-absorbed, too obsessed with my own problems to pay attention to anyone else. I thought I'd had it rough growing up with Dad. But at least I'd *had* him. What a mind blower it was to taste other people's tragedies and to discover, as I had with Fernando, that in the middle of just about anything, it is possible to find a kernel of joy. He had been mine. I couldn't forget what he had said about the men who tortured him: "You love them because they're part of your life, and you love your life." I had begun to love my life now. That was the difference Fernando had made. That's what had happened to me since the night Fernando and I took our Christmas Eve ride on the beach, and we stopped at the rock jetties to watch our faces fill with light. I'd seen myself in him, and I knew that he had seen himself in me. He was still there in memory, a living, growing thing.

Coming out of the parking lot, I hit a speed-breaker, and the glove compartment flew open like it always did. I was about to slam it shut, when I saw that something was taped inside. I pulled the Jeep to the curb. It was a photo of a dark-eyed little girl. I peeled the tape away and picked the photo up. The girl was wearing a white dress with flowers embroidered at the neck. She looked to be less than two years old. The photo itself was creased and dog-eared, as if it had been carried in a wallet and taken out often. On the back was a note in Spanish, but I knew even then what it said: "I had to return to El Salvador, April. A father should be with his daughter. I hope you understand."

I do.